THE BLOOD OF A DRAGON

The Adventures of Thesso and Tarkin

DAWN LA PUMA

A catalogue record for this
book is available from the
National Library of Australia

ISBN 978-0-6450329-4-9(paperback)
ISBN 978-0-6450329-5-6(e-book)

THE BLOOD OF A DRAGON

TABLE OF CONTENTS

CHARACTERS

Humans

Tarkin	From Village of Ainslia Dragon/Human
Kalae	Young female Warrior of Ainslia and Tarkin's Betrothed
Karmen	Tarkin's Daughter
Lase	Tarkin's Son
Eske	Tarkin's Son
Therron	Senior Servant in Dragon cavern.
King Elgrade and King Elgrade 2nd	Ruler of the city of Cam
Jakovyr	King Elgrade's Military Chief
Aurora	Scry, Medium, Sorcerer – working for King Elgrade

Sea Dragons

Thesso	Overseer of the Eastern Oceans
Jodaw	Overseer of the North Seas
Francesca	Overseer of the Western Oceans
Jakeus	Overseer of the Southern Oceans

Dragons in Diamond Cavern

Josepheos	Elder Male
Shari	Elder Female
Miriam	Their young Daughter

Dwarfs

Dwarf King of Christiana	Paelion
Leader of the Dragon Quest.	Thornfoot
King Paelion's Senior advisor	Graynor
Moon Ray	Chief of King Paelion's Personal Guard
Dwarf King of Joannamere	Lombrox

The Team of Dwarfs Chosen to take the Perilous Journey to Find the Dragons.

Thornfoot	Warrior. Strategic Warfare and Leader of Quest.
Hegel	Warrior. Strategic Warfare
Elzer	Warrior. Vision. Spiritual connection to the energies
Elkfast	Warrior. Speed
Treeturn	Warrior. Shape changer. The ability to commune with nature.
Dwaymoon	Warrior Herbalist and Healer
Myrtle	Warrior Recorder of events. Keeper of Histories.
Frurose	Warrior Healer Astral Projection. Shape changer.
Pria	Warrior. Persuader. The Gift of Compulsion

Elves

Caro — Elder in Elf Community, Herbalist and Bows Woman.

Eisvold — Elder in Elf Community, Warrior, Councillor

Metungians

Yanji — Elder in Metumia

Charlotte — Elder in Metumia

Tanir — Animal Handler in Cam's Army. Citizen of Metumia

Tranzicons

Minna — Spokesperson for Transicons

Tomas — Spokesperson and leader of the Tranzicons' Army

The Euradi — A small groups of beings from the dimension called Radi

Nerrens — A group of reptilian people from the Planet Nerra

Hunti — Energetic beings from the land of the Sun Dancers. Evil beings.

Sun Dancers — Inhabitants of one of the regions of space between worlds and dimensions.

Places

Pardow	A Small Orb on which our story takes place.
Ainslia	Tarkin's home village
The Dwarf Kingdom	
Christiana	Home of the Elan Clan and King Paelion
The Dwarf city of Joannamere	Home of King Lombrox and members of Clan Elan
The Kingdom of Cam	Home of King Elgrade the 2nd and the Dragon Cavern
Realm of Aeon	Beyond the veil, An ancient realm
Igiasta	World where the Scarob metal is found.
World of Sun dancers	A World between Worlds a place of energy and movement
Metumia	Home of Metungians
Trantia Mountains	Earthly home and refuge of Metungians
Tranzia	Original Home of the Tranzicons
Den Dargo	Enchanted Forest. Current home of the Tranzicons
Kriea	Home of the Dragons
Nerra	Home of the Nerrens
Radi	Home of the Euradi

PREAMBLE.

When we pick up a book and begin to read a story, we assume we are at the beginning of the story, but in truth no story ever goes all the way back to its true beginning, and no story ever is finished. Countless lifetimes, years of births and deaths, a multitude of civilisations, begun and destroyed or abandoned, go before us. This story is a miniscule series of events that happened on the planet Pardow somewhere in time and space. Pardow was home to an assortment of species, all began their lives, either on a different world or planet, or in another time or dimension. A good deal had arrived via the Portal, and they had chosen to stay, while others were trapped when the Portal closed. There were groups that had chosen to travel to Pardow, as their old civilizations collapsed around them, and they had sought a new homeland.

Pardow is a small, it could be described as tiny, Orb that is part of the Milky Way Galaxy, found in the Scutuna – Centaurus arm, one of the inner arms of the galaxy, and at least, twenty thousand light years from the centre. It is blessed with two vibrant suns, one, which it orbits each day and a second sun which orbits both Pardow and the first sun on a wider trajectory. This second larger sun is visible from Pardow twenty-four hours a day and makes it a very unusual and pretty planet. The evening star clusters are dense and bright, and they along with the second sun, provide light to the night sky in the absence of a moon. This made it a curiosity and attractive to visitors from diverse and unusual places, these visitors brought all sorts of things along with them and thus there was a great diversity of plants and creatures on the land. When the Portal was open centuries ago the species travelled freely throughout the Galaxy, Pardow was a sort after venue for a day out. The plants and pets they brought along with them were introduced to Pardow, but they had been on Pardow for so long now that most inhabitants thought of them as indigenous to the planet.

PREFACE

He gave the horse its head, relying now on the love and trust that they shared to keep her racing forward. The speed and the track were treacherous, but he dared not slow down, the horse also sensed this, and she gave her all, running with urgency and as fast as she could, sweat ran down both their backs and fear raced through their veins. They were one as they raced up the side of the volcano. Shale flew up from the horse's hooves and crashed behind them, but the horse was steady on her feet and did not stumble, her hoofs struck the ground with furious intent. They could hear their pursuers below and behind, but fate was on their side and the top was in sight.

The mountain sensed their fear and cried out, red flames belched up from the summit and rivers of lava began to pour down the mountain side. Right on cue the volcano was erupting. This was great news for the protection of the Chest he was carrying. The contents of the chest were of utmost importance; indeed, they held the key to life or death for all of them.

Leaping from the horse's back Tarkin plunged forward, lurching on his feet as he fought to gain traction on the shale under his feet, he ran hard, desperate to reach the top, his own safety of no importance now, once the Chest was flung into the volcano it did not matter what became of him. Breathing heavily, he threw the Chest with all his might. The Chest glistened red in the light of the volcanic fire and beams of light fell across Tarkin and on to the dragon scale he wore on a thong around his neck. Tarkin wrapped his fingers around the scale and prayed for himself and those he was protecting. He felt energy surge through him, and he raced back to the horse and sprang aboard. The horse needed no urging to begin the descent down the mountain away from the fire, rocks, and lava. Unfortunately, this same path led them to their pursuers. There would be no mercy from the Hunti when they knew they had failed to obtain the chest, and that it was no longer attainable to them. Even as he rode, he could feel their hatred and rage turning toward him as they perceived the Chest, and its power was lost to them.

There was only one thing Tarkin desired, but it seemed an impossibility. If he could reach the ocean and Thesso, the Great Ocean Serpent, he may survive. His chances were not good as the Hunti closed on him. He grabbed at the scale around his neck, holding it for courage, felt its smooth edges and the sharp sides, felt his flesh slicing. Strangely now he felt as if he was drowning. Water wrapped around him, it felt warm and soothing, he relaxed into the feeling of weightlessness and the sensation of falling, and his consciousness left him.

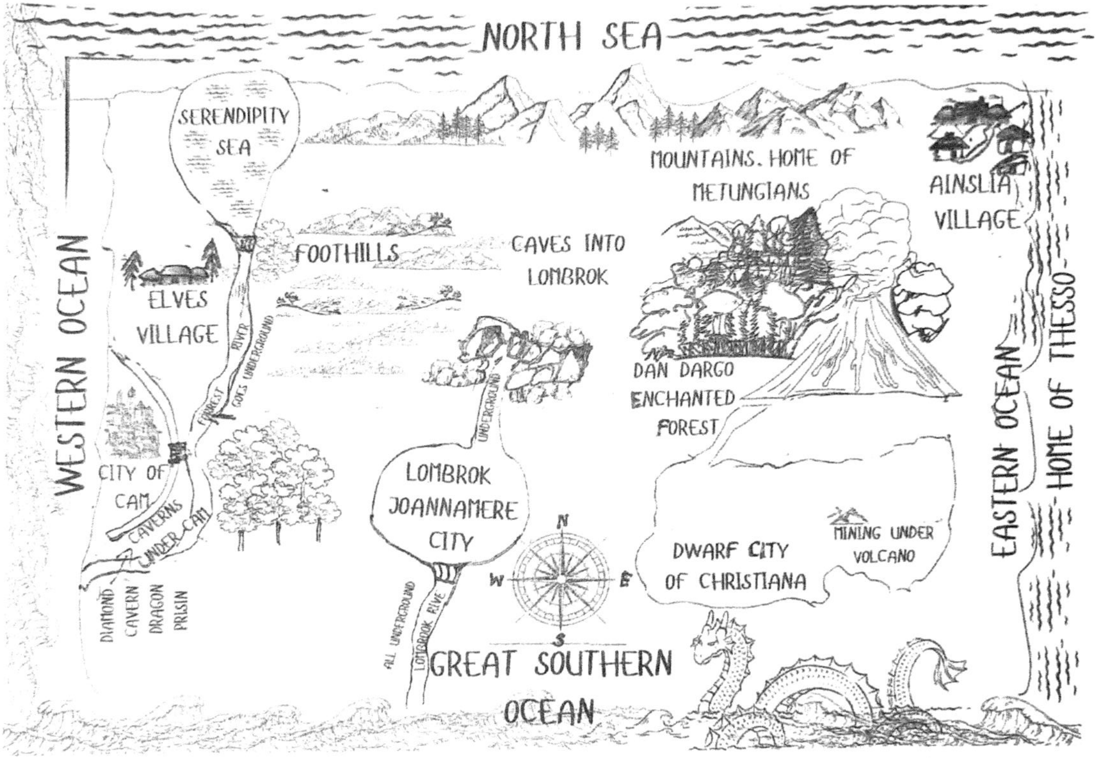
NORTH SEA
SERENDIPITY SEA
MOUNTAINS. HOME OF METUNGIANS
AINSLIA VILLAGE
WESTERN OCEAN
ELVES VILLAGE
FOOTHILLS
CAVES INTO LOMBROK
FORREST RIVER
GOES UNDERGROUND
UNDERGROUND
DAN DARGO ENCHANTED FOREST
CITY OF CAM
CAVERNS UNDER CAM
DIAMOND CAVERN DRAGON PRISIN
LOMBROK JOANNAMERE CITY
N
W
E
S
DWARF CITY OF CHRISTIANA
MINING UNDER VOLCANO
EASTERN OCEAN
HOME OF THESSO
ALL UNDERGROUND
LOMBROOK RIVE
GREAT SOUTHERN OCEAN

PART ONE

FIRST ENCOUNTER

Tarkin began his morning meditation in the usual way. He expected nothing more than to experience the loss of self and to become one with the universe. He spread his reed mat on the soft white sand just above the wave line. He breathed in the scent of the giant trees that lined the beach and looked for a long time to the mountain peaks that towered over him. Each morning, he gave thanks to his God for the place he lived and for his life. He did not question God, or who or what that meant. He accepted that he often felt a power that he could not explain so he simply accepted this was God or at least the essence of God.

He gave thanks for his parents and family for the land they worked and for the village and villagers around about them, the sea for its provision of food. Then he began to expand his mind. He allowed his conscious mind to slip away and began to draw on the universal energy that flows in, through and around all of us. so that not only did he exist here on the beach, but he existed in a sense of timelessness, an all-encompassing present, where he was one with everything and everyone.

In this meditative state he was the energy. He drew the energy through his body and imagined it flowing through every one of his cells and then he allowed the energy to pour from him and expand until it covered everything around him. He pushed this energy out further and further, imagining the mountains and beyond and the people that he knew and to those he didn't, upward and outward the energy travelled, and he listened to the voices of the world, to the sounds of the universe, to the words of the Gods. He was one with all these things.

What he did not know or understand was his universe was so much larger than even he imagined and that there were creatures, places, and dimensions he had no knowledge of. Today he would experience the first seeds of this possibility because a truly magnificent creature was observing him. This tiny human had caught the attention of Thesso the sea dragon. Tarkin was completely unaware of this but today his life would change forever.

Thesso was a formidable creature, a terrific and remarkable sight. He was around nine metres long with a strongly muscled body that was dragon-like at the top. His huge head was also that of a dragon. His scales were every colour of the rainbow, this colour was magnified by the water pouring from them as he thrust his huge body up from the depths of the ocean. They shimmered blindingly in the sunlight. His body, which was shaped like a huge snake, tapered off gently to a huge fish like tail and he had small wings just below his head. These wings were for balance as he did not fly, they were made of gossamer, a brilliant turquoise that flashed in the sun. Although the wings were not made for flying, they seemed to aid in the effortless movement of the great beast through the water as he moved through the waves with smooth undulations of his muscular body. His arms and legs were quite small in comparison to his size, but, like the wings, he used them infrequently. If he had to go on dry land, they were helpful. He rarely did venture out of the ocean.

Thesso had felt the vibrations of Tarkin's mind before, it had been weak and Thesso had not thought to query what or who it was. He knew it was human energy that he was sensing, and he knew that man was a creature who, no longer committed to the spiritual paths of their ancestors. Most had lost or forgotten their spiritual side. As the young man's energy gained strength Thesso felt it more clearly, he began to pay attention. Thesso sensed this young man was different.

Humankind existed entirely in the physical realm, relying on their senses of sight, hearing, touch, and taste, to relate to the world around them and to gather information from it. Even physical senses were becoming duller as man related to what he could see, feel, and touch. What he believed to be truth was what he had been taught by his parents, and these ideas and beliefs were passed on to the next generation. Very few men ever questioned what they had been taught. The spiritual aspects of life were pushed increasingly into the background until they barely existed.

As Thesso spent time studying Tarkin he observed that he used his senses to see the world around him but also, he had an understanding of other senses he could access and use. He was learning how his physical self was intensely connected with his spiritual self, he wanted to expand his knowledge, but this was not a time of spirituality, and the teachings and the knowledge of such things were all but lost. Searching for a connection had led to Tarkin's days of quiet meditation on the beach, to the expansion of his mind, to a connection point with the greater universal energy. Tarkin may have felt alone in the vastness of the universal energies, but he most definitely was not.

Thesso, the great ocean dragon, continued watching Tarkin with curiosity, as he did his interest in the young man increased. Thesso was one of the four great ocean dragons; he was the dragon of, and the guardian of, the Eastern Oceans. His physical power was immense as was his spiritual power. His connection to all made him a most powerful life form. There were few to match him in the universe. There was no way to compare the mind power of Thesso or his physical and spiritual power with that of the human youth.

He, like the dragons of all four corners of the earth, ocean keepers, had the power to control the seas and thus the weather and the fortune of all life forms on the planet Pardow. Common to all dragons, land sea and air, are powers of the mind. They exchanged knowledge and by the linking of their thoughts with one another they communicated over distance and time. They all had their own distinctive powers and gifts. The ocean dragons were shape changers, they were a ridiculously small number of creatures that had this skill. Each had specific gifts which enhanced the power of the four, Thesso could entwine spiritually with other life forms thus endowing other physical bodies with all the strength, knowledge, and spiritual gifts he himself had. In this state he was able to access himself of any powers and attributes of the other life form. The use of this gift required the use of physical power and mental power, it also required the ability to control and direct the spiritual energies. The shifting, or manipulation, of the energies caused repercussions across space, time, and dimensions. Something was usually taken or had to be given up in return for the use of such power.

Meanwhile, Thesso and the youth continued their individual paths, Thesso observed Tarkin as he continued his daily meditative practices. Thesso's curiosity began to increase as he felt the clear, clean, searching energy of the youth as he sought answers to all the questions that taunted his mind every day. Thesso longed for companionship, to be able to converse on a level of spiritual intellect was something he craved for, here was one who would be willing to learn. He decided, the next time Tarkin was meditating and thus available for him to reach, the two would meet mind to mind.

The next morning when Tarkin came to the beach to meditate Thesso was waiting close by. He kept well out of sight under water and when he sensed Tarkin he began to expand his mind, and he reached out and extended his energy field toward that of the young man. He felt the excitement in the youth's energy field as it experienced the connection with his own vastly stronger energetic force. He felt the weaker human's immediate, terrified reaction and felt his fear jolt him into consciousness. Thesso was annoyed with himself, he should have been more subtle. He would be more careful next time and not frighten the lad; his power was too much for Tarkin to interact with straight away. Thesso vowed to keep it in check and try again. He would not make the same mistake next time. He already felt a connection with, and affection for, the youth.

On the beach Tarkin's eyes flew open and he came back to the reality around him. He understood he had connected with a powerful being. After his initial shock he began to think everything through, and he realised that this was what he had been wanting for a long time. His fear fell away, and he was excited with the connection but annoyed at his own withdrawal. He remembered the sheer power and force of the energy field and he realised his withdrawal was self-preserving. He must be ready next time, he shivered at the thought, he would do his best not to react this way next time their minds met. He packed his things and walked back up the beach. He was excited but he knew he must get back to his work and he also knew that he would be better for the contemplation and the wait. Self-discipline was one of his characteristics.

TARKIN

Tarkin lived on the shores of a great ocean, so large there was no other visible land point that anyone could see in any direction. He lived in a small village called Ainslia. There was a story attached to this name, but he could not remember it. Here, on the planet Pardow, there was a story attached to everything. Neither he nor anyone he knew had ventured out to sea beyond the sight of the beach around Ainslea. The ocean provided a wonderfully abundant source of food for the villagers nestled on its shores. Fish were abundant in the ocean and the villagers either caught them on lines from shore or from their small crafts. Sometimes fish became trapped in the large rock holes after an especially high tide and could be easily caught by hand. It appeared as if the ocean favoured the village. The villagers often sailed their small boats for pleasure, they swam and played in the green waters that washed the shore, but they were land dwellers. They had everything they needed here. There was no need for any changes. No one felt the need to explore wider fields. It seemed that no one except Tarkin himself was interested in what was across the water or anywhere else.

Tarkin had grown up in this tiny hamlet, nestled between the mountains and the ocean. One of these mountains was so high you rarely glimpsed the top as it was often wreathed in clouds. Occasionally fire and smoke belched from the mountain, but it never made its way down to the bottom. The soil at the foot of the mountain was fertile and the land teemed with vegetation. There were various creatures that lived among the verdant growth, but nothing harmed the people. Farmers grew their crops in peace and were sure of their yield. All the necessities of life were right here. There were never any arguments or disputes in the village as there was nothing to argue about. Life was simple here on the water's edge.

Growing up in this idyllic, laconic way, Tarkin would have agreed he loved his life, but he was always curious, always craving more understanding. To know what lay beyond the ocean that stretched endlessly before him, he wanted to understand what else lived in the ocean? What lay beyond the mountains, where does the wind come from, where does it go? Childish curiosity at first but it grew with him to a level of frustration that resulted in a restlessness that he kept well-hidden. The years never answered these questions, and his frustrations were mostly ignored by everyone except Kalae. She listened to him and when they were younger, they had made up stories together to answer the questions. As she got older, she became increasingly satisfied with her everyday life. She looked forward to being a wife, having children and carrying on in blissful harmony with Tarkin here in the village. Despite this she maintained an interest in the spiritual side of life. As Tarkin continued his meditative practices, she would spend time learning and growing herself in these ways. It was something they did together and having her with him calmed his frustrations. There were few answers in the village and Tarkin knew he had to be resigned to wait and learn what and where he could.

In his seventeenth year Tarkin was looking forward to his union with Kalae, the love of his life. They had been committed to each other on the night of their birth as was the custom. He had never questioned this commitment, and the very fabric of his life was woven around it. Kalae was born minutes after he was, in the same hut, on the same table and with the same midwife. Their mothers had joined them while their own blood was still on the babies and on the table, Tarkin and Kalae had been inseparable all their lives.

Kalae was dark skinned like Tarkin, she had beautiful, deep brown hair, which grew to her waist. Her hair was always braided, close to her head, and she decorated the braids with ribbons and flowers the same way all the village woman and girls did. Tarkin never tired of the sight of her. He looked forward to meeting her each day and experiencing the pleasure that wrapped around him as she smiled.

He too was dark skinned, and he was tall, standing head and shoulders over his parents which was a source of pride to them. Healthy food, love and exercise were the perfect recipe for a perfect man, or so they claimed. Tarkin's head was clean shaven except for the middle of his head where the hair was left to become a single braid from his forehead to the nape of his neck and longer down his back. The plaited part that fell down his back was wrapped and decorated with leather thong and various beads and small stones. He was lean and muscular with the youthful promise of a strong physique when he reached full maturity. Tarkin and Kalae were almost identical to every other couple in the village.

THESSO AND
THE PORTAL

Thesso was centuries old and had sought knowledge throughout his life. He believed that knowledge gathered and held, gave insight and power. His vast knowledge was gained via observing, listening, genetic transfer of memories, the readings of other dragons. He read and listened to the minds and voices of all life forms; he also travelled the vast seas of this world. He travelled the air and land by using the physical form of other animals and birds and humans.

In the past he had also travelled the Portal – the Portal which for aeons he had held the secret to. Centuries ago, he had joined with the most arcane powers of the universe to create a different form of travel. They had created a Portal using these powers to force open pathways between worlds, dimensions and to allow movement of physical form along these paths that led the way between the separate worlds and dimensions. To be able to move without the limitation of time and space was an incredible thing. Anyone who travelled along these paths had increased their knowledge and understanding of the world they lived in. They realised there were worlds that were inhabited by beings so unlike themselves it was hard to believe. This learning helped all to understand their own minds, to be tolerant of differences and to feel the connection between all things. This Portal was enjoyed and used by all beings. There were no restrictions, and everyone went where and when they pleased. Soon there was a prevailing harmonic energy along the pathways.

To connect with all around you must first know that much more exists than that which one sees, hears, and feels. Soon anyone, anywhere, who wished, could use the Portal. The Portal provided a sense of oneness throughout the universes, an understanding that all were connected, thus harmony was achieved throughout the vast number of worlds and dimensions. This harmony lasted for a long time, but it did not last forever.

As Thesso's affection and trust for Tarkin grew he began to talk to him about the Portal and how it was used and its power, and how people had originally loved it, but had eventually abused it, bringing disharmony and fear to the pathways. The creators of this amazing Portal felt they had no choice so because of this anger and division they had made the difficult decision to close the pathways. They were no longer able to support its open availability to all.

The Portal would be missed and indeed Thesso missed it right now. He tried to teach Tarkin about the worlds around him. 'In the realm or worlds where humans live, it is sometimes, always, their belief that this planet is alone in the universe. The thought that there is nothing else, that stories of Gods are just made up to give us something to believe in, to satisfy our minds that there is no other species.' They proclaim, 'God made us! That is all there is! Now we struggle to even conceive God.' He continued, 'Tarkin we are one tiny world in the vast web of worlds, one of a vastness beyond your comprehension. Even when you try to understand and embrace this truth you cannot.

For you, right now, it is simply enough to accept what you are a part of this universe, this connectivity.'

Thesso began to play with an idea. Thesso understood that the life span of man was short unlike other species that lived for hundreds of years, so attaining a knowledge of all things was a challenging and difficult path for a human. He began to contemplate the idea of reopening the Portals to access the secret pathways, to allow Tarkin to walk them with him throughout the universe. The pathways were a vast network of roads that surpassed time, dimension, and space, an energetic series of pathways, a road to new worlds and old ones, of endless discovery, a source of limitless knowledge. Thesso decided to seek permission to reopen the Portal.

He explained this thought to Tarkin, 'Remember I told you that there was a Portal between world and dimensions, and this Portal operated outside of time and space. It is held together by the combined will of all major spiritual beings in all the dimensions, times, and places, past, present, and future. It is a vortex in which time and space is not present. Within the Portal the physical form is changed to the energetic thus allowing movement to wherever the traveller wishes to be. Within the Portal time stands still'

'The Portal was created by the highest levels of consciousness to allow all beings to move freely and quickly between the worlds, a way to travel and study and to gain knowledge. A means to understanding the connection between all things and the understanding of life and self. To connect with all one must first be aware that he or she is part of all things, there is so much more than that which one experiences in the physical. There is so much more to discover than that which is seen, heard, and felt.'

THE HUNTI AND
THE SUNDANCERS

During the time that the Portal was open to all, there was a wonderful harmonious state between all the different species, this wonderful period of harmony continued for many thousands of years, but unfortunately everything was about to change as in the world of the Sundancers there was an evil growing.

Let me tell you about the Sundancers. Sundancers were exactly as their name suggested. They danced in the sun. Their world, a small world that existed within the plains, between dimensions, was lit by seven glorious suns, these suns never went down. The suns provided the energy for the dancers and the dancers used the energy, thus everything remained in balance. The dancers never slept, they simply danced, as they absorbed energies and warmth from the air around them. They made love and reproduced in the rhythm of the dance. Life, birth, death was a rhythmic movement.

Over years the energy from the Sundancers constant movement was more than they were able to reabsorb. Other energetic organisms and beings began to form, and when these energetic beings got out of rhythm with their fellow dancers they were rejected and ostracised. Anyone different to the Sundancers, and uncoordinated with the rhythm of the dance were pushed out of the mainstream and to the edges of society. To the edge of the dance. One group of these new energetic beings, lived in the place of the dead where Sundancers who had reached the end of their life cycle and no longer danced, could be left to be burned up and eventually consumed by the suns. Here they fed on the energies of any grief and mourning along with the natural energy left over from the dancer. Just as they were shunned and tormented by the Sundancers they began to enjoy tormenting the Sundancers as they danced their weak and dying out, to this place. They began to taunt the dancers who were always in a hurry, wanting nothing more than to dance back to their place in the rhythm. This annoyance produced anger, which created negative energy for the new beings to absorb. When a ball of energy became too large it would split into fragments and each fragment began to collect negativity and grow until it too would split. Thus, their numbers increased rapidly. They became known as the evil ones, or the Hunti.

Every now and then a visitor using the Portal came across this amazing and beautiful place between worlds and although they were mesmerised at first, they soon began to burn, they left as quickly as they had come and one day the Hunti went with them.

The Hunti had no physical shape, and they travelled as they lived, as energetic bodies. Their energy bodies melded with the energy around them. They began to seek out places to feed their need for negative energies and when none was found they began to create them. As the Hunti became stronger they began to use the Portal regularly to feed. This was necessary to live. There was not enough negativity to feed off at home as they had grown in number and the Sundancers felt little other than the, all compelling, need to dance.

The Hunti needed to find a bigger source of negative energy, and they had learnt that anger and discontent fuelled their growth and power. Finding this energy was only possible in a place of emotion and passion. The Sundancers were not an emotional race and accepted the death of other flowers with a fleeting sadness. Their need to keep the rhythm was overwhelming.

MANGARA

The Hunti travelled continuously along the pathways. They had the ability to manipulate emotion and thus caused normally happy beings to feel sadness or anger. They could also use this energy to manipulate the minds of those around them, causing them to hallucinate and see what was not there. This way they induced creatures to turn on each other as if their friend were a horrifying beast set to murder them. The energy produced by the Hunti could cause extreme pain in the heads of their victim, this caused them to go mad and then they too were a danger to those around them. The Hunti loved this result. Negativity drew negativity and the Hunti did not hesitate to draw attention to themselves. They did not know how to be discreet. It was in the Portal that they first came upon Mangara. Mangara was an ancient sorcerer, powerful and revered at one time, but as he became older, he became less and less popular, he became unstable to the eyes of those around him. He sought power and he wanted to be in complete control of everything and everyone that crossed his path. He had been thrust aside by his peers because of what was seen as madness and this thought was enhanced by the crazy ideas and thoughts on magic and the ethereal that he continuously sprouted. He came from a world that was more metaphysical than physical. This was a world of shadow, of forgotten or stolen thoughts. Memories taken by stealth and used to create magic. The world did exist, but it only existed when you knew it did. This is how it remained a mystery and remained safe from interference. Once Mangara lost his power over his world he began to travel the pathways to different worlds, he used the Portal, often searching for beings to extort and manipulate to get them to help him in his quest and his passion for lost artifacts, or perceived, lost artifacts.

Mangara was drawn to the Hunti as they too were etherical rather than physical, and they loved negativity. Despite the fact the Hunti were not able to physically attack anything, they were extremely dangerous as the energies that surrounded them caused all sorts of negative responses. They were by nature cruel and enjoyed the pain of others. When confronted by the energetic force of the Hunti other beings would turn on each other in their fear and confusion and cause injuries they never would have conceived themselves capable of. In the same way anyone around Mangara was also susceptible to his supernatural power. When Mangara was in the Portal he would manipulate the minds of the other travellers so that they would become sad or angry. A memory of a lost love or a murdered child evoked strong emotion, he stole these emotions and the Hunti fed on the aftermath of anger or sadness. This added to their own negative energies and their pushing and pulling, by expanding and contracting their energy fields, always generated negative energy for them to feed on. They started to follow wherever Mangara travelled and thus they came to be codependent. Mangara knew other misfits travelling the pathways and the number of evil entities increased. As they grew in numbers and strength, their needs and desires also grew, and greater acts of harm and pain were caused by them. Soon disharmony reigned between the species using the energetic roads.

THE FIRST CLOSING
OF THE PORTAL

U nable to ignore the unrest and distress being caused within the Portal the Higher Consciousness realised there was no choice but to close it. At first, they felt they should dissolve the Portal, but the energy required to do so was extreme and it would be unlikely it could ever be reopened if a time came when they felt it right to do so. A conference was held in the upper echelons of Consciousness and the four great Sea Dragons were called to confer. It was at this conference the decision for Thesso to take and control of the Portal was made. The access to the Portal was formed in the shape of a small disc, not unlike a dragon's scale. Thesso was to take and hide this disc which now held the Portal access for better times if they were ever reemergent, and he agreed to do so. He hid the Portal in the vast oceans and for centuries it had remained safely hidden.

The dragons were the most powerful of the physical beings and the four of them ruled the four seas of Pardow and thus held sway over all corners of the planet. Great hurricanes formed on the ocean surfaces, and they controlled the climate. Not only this, but Pardow's rivers also were cleaned by the oceans and food and transport was provided to humans and other earthly creatures. Minerals and chemicals were found in their depths. All life forms depended on the oceans and the oceans depended on the Dragons. Thesso, the guardian of the Eastern Seas was the most powerful of the four Dragons. He mastered the Eastern Seas which were the strongest and roughest because of their physical position on the planet. More people were affected by the eastern oceans than any of the other oceans. Thesso had been given the position of ruler of the great Eastern Sea eons ago. He was the oldest and strongest of the dragons of the four seas. Jodaw ruled the North Sea and Francesca ruled the Western Oceans. Jakeus ruled the great Southern Oceans. All four were significantly powerful beings.

On the sad, but inevitable, day came when it was time to close the Portal. There was a vast number of beings trapped in realms, times, and places, other than their own. Warnings and times of the closure had been given over and over to prevent this happening. Every effort was made to prevent this outcome but the vastness of the pathways and the myriads of beings from all worlds, times and dimensions had made it almost inevitable that there would be those who did not understand or would simply miscalculate the time. Others simply chose to stay where they were for reasons of their own. The Hunti were among those who decided to stay on Pardow where they were, as did Mangara and his followers. Those left behind, either by choice or by chance, had simply found a place to live and over the decades they had died out, their forms and stories now forgotten here in this world. The groups were had most probably been hunted by the frightened humans, the main inhabitants of Pardow, as they feared the unknown and thus these new arrivals would have been lost as a species here. There were also other groups who quickly realised their predicament and had opted for concealment.

THE METUNGIANS

This was what happened to the Metungians, a large group from Metumia, a world far removed but not unsimilar to this one. On hearing of the impending closure of the Portal they decided to come to Pardow for a final picnic. They wanted to hike up into the mountains and have their meal and play games. Coming to visit Pardow always amused them as the main inhabitants were so tiny that it made them feel like giants. There had been weeks of communications passed on to them by their leaders, that the Portal was to be closed. With all of this in mind a group of Metungians decided to make a final journey in the Portal, they wanted it to be one of significance and to be adventurous. The group consisted of younger men and women, young families, and older family members, grandmothers, and grandfathers. There were about sixty in the group. They were all fit and well.

Although they knew that the Portal was closing, they made a serious miscalculation of the timing despite having a calculation device that moved sand through a tube with them. Getting mixed up with time was easy as time is non-existent in the Portal so while they had travelled via the Portal, and it was open for them to return, they were in the vortex that was the Portal, when it closed that energy dissipated and time began to move forward for them.

As soon as they felt the Portal close, they realised their mistake and the consequences of it. They were now cut off. They could not return home. Without the Portal it was impossible. Crying and panic ensued, no one really knew what to do or how to react. Here they were, on a strange planet, one they knew little about except it was not their home. Their homeland was one that relied on technology. Pardow, they knew was not as advanced in this area. Their communications devises did not work here. That was one of the reasons they liked it. It was so much more peaceful. After some time, where the older people in the group managed to calm the younger ones down, they decided to continue hiking farther up into the mountains, the ranges were not so high and thus easier to climb, for them as they were about three times as large as a human. They were a handsome and well-muscled people with natural strength and speed. They knew that the humans would fear them because of their superior size so they decided that they would be better off to remain separated from other beings on the planet for a while so that they could consider their situation and work out what to do next.

They had hiked a long way into the Trantia mountains after the Portal closed. They knew there was a flat area they had used as a recreation ground before, so they had been seeking it for their games and picnic. The Trantia mountain range had, years before, been struck by a meteor which had dug a deep crater into the side of the mountain. The meteor had formed a perfect environment for plants and trees and there were creeks and big rivers flowing across the crater. Plants of all sorts grew in the cracks and crevasses in the walls of the crater, birds were in abundance and small animals could be heard scuttling away as they approached. Three sides of the crater were within the mountain range, steep walls had been cut out of the side of the mountains, these walls would be hard to scale unnoticed. On the Northern side the crater faced the North Sea where huge cliffs fell into the ocean and relentless waves pounded their feet. No beach, and no inhabitants! A perfect hideaway! The Metungians sat down and began to talk, the facts were obvious, they had to stay on this world. Pardow was where they would live for now. How long they would have to stay here on Pardow was unknown.

They talked of how, and where, they would find shelter. As they looked around at the area, they were in, they quickly realised this would be the best place to start their life on this new world. The position and the heavy forestation sheltered birds and other wildlife. Ideal for providing food and shelter. There were various species of plants and grasses which they hoped would prove valuable for medicines and food. They wasted no time getting established, they began by setting up small, individual shelters, using what they found in the forest, they gathered firewood and sought out edible plants. They were all aware that their picnic supplies would not last long.

As they days slowly passed the shock of their situation was wearing off. They decided to see what they had with them that may be useful. Everything was set out in the centre of the group for all to see and it was accessed as to how it may be used to help them set up and create a life for themselves. Mobile phones, torches, mechanical toys, watches, and all metal jewellery was put into a pile. There was no way to power any of these devices here. They would have to work out how to recreate a power source. The more mechanical and technical Metungians were assigned to work on this task. They would study the items before them to find ways to use them here in their new world. If that were not possible, they would use them for parts and inspiration to create things that would be of benefit to them.

Finding a power source for light would be the first thing on which they would work. Once they had an idea of what was needed, they would have to find a source for it. One that was accessible to them here on Pardow. This was to be their new home, and it was important that they accepted this and got to work of making a place for themselves.

Everyone agreed, even the younger ones, that one thing that should be established was an education system for the children and young adults in the group. Metungians were used to an elevated level of education on their home planet of Metumia and the elders thought it important to keep teaching these skills to the younger generation. The history of, and everything about their home planet, was to be passed down as well. But first things first, they had to focus on the necessities of day-to-day life to ensure their survival and their good health. Once the settlement was functioning smoothly, they would then turn to these longer-term plans.

The Metungians worked continuously on their inventions, they concentrated on those they missed most like cooking devises and lights, machines to wash the clothing and they needed better dwellings, over time they managed to find a source of hard metal by using the magnets from the toys. It was necessary to create a furnace to melt this metal down, but after this it opened new paths for them.

After a time getting settled in and coming to an acceptance of the planet as their home, they began to send out scouts to see what was out in the larger community that they might learn from and use in the development of their own village. They soon realised that they were well advanced in technical knowledge and felt they could learn nothing of this sort from the planet's other inhabitants but felt that they could share their own ideas with them. This did not prove easy as the humans treated them with suspicion and were afraid of their superior size.

The group had found a perfect hideaway and as they were mostly young and healthy they were able to reproduce and now years later there was a thriving populations and community with businesses and infrastructure. It was by now a well well-established and prosperous city. The Metungians had created a system of leadership and advisors just as they had had at home.

THE PORTAL
REOPENS

D ecades passed, generations came and went, and the Portal was not reopened. Over time the species' lifestyles changed, and they lived in harmony with the planet and their neighbours. But there were those that were not content! The Hunti had deliberately stayed on Pardow; they did not want to return to the land of the Sundancers where they had originated. The Sundancers' carefree disposition gave them little negative energy to feed on. This world suited them better, the inhabitants here were disagreeable and felt pain easily. The humans grieved their dead. They argued and fought bitter wars. They were jealous and filled with envy. They desired what was not theirs. It was a good place for a Hunti to thrive.

Over time the wars became less and less, people began to enjoy the peace, and more contentment was found among the people. Lovely little villages, like Ainslia, sprang up and the villagers lived in harmony with their neighbours. This of course, had a negative effect on the Hunti, and they grew weaker. They desperately missed the days when they could move freely through the pathways of the Portal seeking minds and physical bodies to exploit. Mangara continued to help them by creating what disharmony and emotional grief that he could. He urged them over and over to find the Portal and then with him in control of it, they would have power over everything and everyone.

Years came and passed, and nothing disturbed the peace which continued to reign throughout the lands and worlds, dimensions, and times. Thesso and Tarkin grew in friendship and trust and Thesso wanted to share more knowledge with him. By now they remained connected mind to mind all the time and the two shared each other's thoughts. Each was acutely aware of the other no matter how far or how long they spent apart. One day as the Portal became part of the conversation. Tarkin asked Thesso for more information as he did not have a full understanding of the Portal and lacked full knowledge of what it did and how it worked.

Thesso recognised the myriads of things Tarkin had no experience with, or knowledge of, and he decided to try to reopen the Portal. To do this he would need the consent of those who had made it. This was not an easy argument to win, and it took long and arduous conversations, vigorous persuading, and endless debating. The argument Thesso had used was simple, if he wanted to change mankind's thinking, and Tarkin was a man, humankind needed knowledge and that the time needed to learn could be reduced by travelling the pathways. If Tarkin was allowed even one journey on the pathways he could achieve years of advancement in his education.

How could any humans change their thinking when their knowledge was limited to their own lifespan of a mere fifty years. It was a good argument, and the advancement of all creatures was considered worthwhile by the powers controlling the Portal. Eventually the great minds agreed to the re-opening of the Portal. Not everyone was in favour of the reopening but eventually the decision was finalized and Thesso once again was given permission to open and maintain control over the Portal. It was not for everyone this time, only for Thesso and for Tarkin's education. Thesso of course had the full use of the Portal at his discretion. To use the Portal, you now had to have the disc in your possession.

With the help of all the original ones that first created the Portal and the input of other energetic and spiritually powerful beings the Portal was successfully reopened. Tarkin was overawed and overwhelmed by his fear, he trembled with excitement and just a little apprehension. Thesso reassured him, 'The disc can take us through time and space at a thought or the desire to go. We can also explore the dimensions where countless versions of the same world live side by side and on top and below each other. There is more I can tell you, but it takes time to absorb in and even more to comprehend. Imagine the power that having this disc gives to the person in control of it! That is why there was the reluctance to allow the reopening. We have been given an opportunity and a privilege that we must protect it at all costs. You will understand more as time goes on. Do not be apprehensive, we will travel together, until you are comfortable to travel alone,' and so began Tarkin's great adventure and the discovery of worlds and realms. Beyond even his vast imagination.

Tarkin shared all the interesting facts of his travels and shared his stories with Kalae, and she listened intently and enjoyed the tales of far-off places and of places right on top of them but in a different time or dimension. Although Tarkin did ask of Thesso that Kalae be permitted to travel with them Thesso declined. The more people who used the Portal, and who may be noted as simply disappearing for days. could cause other interested parties to be suspicious. He considered it would be safer for them and the Portal if it were only used by the two of them.

Tarkin's adventures on the pathways were unimaginably wonderful. His knowledge increased and he enjoyed the frequent visit to all sorts of worlds, he remembered when he had sat on the beach in his home village of Ainslia and thought, 'there must be more than what I can see and feel.' Well know he knew that there definitely was, and his education and imagination grew day by day, along with it a newfound compassion for all living things.

Tarkin, and therefore, Thesso were blissfully happy. They increased their knowledge of the worlds around them and their respect and love for each other grew. This blissful state would not last forever however as not all was well, not everyone had forgotten the Portal. You can only imagine the pleasure and excitement when Mangara, who was one of the beings who not forgotten the Portal because he was obsessed with it, realised it was open again. His every waking moment was an attempt to find it. He had felt it when it had reopening. He gathered his followers together and gave them the news of what he had felt. The Hunti had felt this energy themselves. The Hunti are entirely composed of energy, so they felt changes, any changes, no matter how subtle, in the energy fields of this world and in other worlds in all the dimensions of time and space. Such a strong disruption was easily sensed. Others had felt it, but not all had recognised what it was. The Hunti did not yet know where the Portal was, and they had no understanding of the fact they could not access it unless Thesso and Tarkin together could be forced to open it for them. They did not know it was now only used with the possession of a certain disc. A disc made from the scale of a dragon. Not an ordinary dragon but the most powerful of all dragons. Despite any concrete knowledge of where to start they followed the trail of the Portal, and they began to search.

Humans and the other physical beings whose ancestors had used the pathways myriads of years before had lost their connection to the spiritual side of themselves. They had no knowledge of the Portal, anything passed down was long forgotten and the religions of the day frowned upon the talk of spiritual matters. Humans felt that they were the dominant species. Any reference to a spiritual side was touted as a weakness and if you were interested in this you were seen as a weakling, The Portal was non-existent in the eyes of the physical worlds. The worlds and people did not recognise the existence of each other. They thought themselves and their own world to be the only one.

After many successful journeys Thesso asked Tarkin if he was ready to travel alone, Tarkin agreed that he was now very comfortable using the Portal so Thesso decided he would give the Portal to Tarkin to use in his absence, he also felt that Tarkin should have the liberty and thus the responsibility of going where and when he pleased. Thesso often liked to travel great distances in the ocean in his role of caretaker of the Great Eastern Ocean. Tarkin still had his family and work to do within the village, so their times did not always correlate. Thesso gave the disc to Tarkin and impressed once more on him the importance of keeping it secure and when not in use to ensure it was locked away in a safe place. This disc was made from the scale that Thesso had given Tarkin a section of previously to help in their connection. It seemed fitting to use the same one in connection with their continuing journey.

Taking every precaution, they decided to construct a Chest in which Tarkin could hold the disc. This Chest would have to be impenetrable. They sought the materials from near and far and finally agreed that the Scarab metal, which is only found on the planet Igiasta where it is a scared metal, formed in the fire of a dragon's breath. This metal is unbreakable unless you are using a tool fashioned from the same metal and in the same way. Tarkin and Thesso sought this metal on one of their journeys along the pathways. They chose Igiasta as it is dimensions and times away from Pardow. One could only reach it via the pathways, and they would have to know that it existed to decide to travel there. Once the Chest was finished the disc was locked inside and a lock was formed that only the minds of Tarkin and Thesso together can open. Thesso was taking no chances on the disc falling into the wrong hands or the Chest being opened by the wrong people. He was taking all these precautions as somewhere in the back or his consciousness something familiar was troubling him. He felt an energy forming, he had not yet recognised his unease but on the edge of his mind a cautionary feeling was growing. Something was stirring.

THE HUNTI
ATTACK AINSLIA
AND ATTACK
MANGARA AND
HIS FOLLOWERS

The Portal had closed years hence, but Mangara was determined to find the pathways again. He had never given up the search for the Portal. When he had it in his possession he would return in time and regain his position of power. Meanwhile he had his cohorts to do his bidding. Here in this world where he had remained at the first closing of the Portal he had, over the years, recruited various followers some of whom were human, these devotees were those that had forgotten their roots and sought only to be happy and to have money and goods. They were easily influenced by the promise of these things. Mangara also had among his followers a strange menagerie of creatures that had stayed with him at the beginning. Mangara induced the humans to follow him, to believe him when he told them about a Portal that would take them to a new world, indeed a myriad of worlds, worlds where they would have all the power and thus have all the riches. He had formed a large following of believers that were extremely happy to listen to his madness. He was a sorcerer, and he had convincing ways of making the gullible believe him to be all powerful. He used his power over their minds to read their dreams and sorrows, and then he used this information to trick them and convince them into believing he was truly a God.

His desire for the Portal, which would ensure a victorious return to his own realm, had not waned over all the years and therefore for these long, fruitless years he had been continually scheming and planning ways to obtain knowledge of its whereabouts. And now he, along with the Hunti, had sensed its reopening and he doubled his efforts to find it. He sent his apostles all over the planet to seek news. The Hunti numbers had been subsiding for decades as the peace did not feed them, but now with this renewed energy they began to grow from strength to strength, they multiplied quickly. Fuelled by anticipation they allowed their rage to grow. They once again inflicted cruel punishment on any being that came across their path. Their actions attracted the attention of other beings that had been silently waiting for this day and evil began to raise its head once more. Opportunity drew them together. There was no love for each other amongst the Hunti or any of the other evil beings and they often took out their anger and negativity on each other. With the Hunti multiplying rapidly Mangara sent out more of his followers to join the hunt for the location of the Portal, to follow the Hunti, who he believed would be able follow the source of the energy coming from the Portal better than any other group could.

About the same time Tarkin was happily travelling the world and imagining his upcoming wedding, he had not perceived that the Hunti were gathering their strength. He had no former knowledge of the Hunti and what they were. You could not see a Hunti, but you could sense them because the air around them was filled with dark energy and evil intent. When you did sense them, your hair stood up on the back of your neck and you shivered with fear and a desire to run filled your being without you knowing why. Thesso was sensing this rise in evil and recognised the Hunti were pursuing the Portal and that they, and others, knew the Portal was open. They had no idea that it was no longer available to them as it had been previously, but even if they had they would not have cared. They wanted to have the Portal and then when they had it in their hands, they would work out what to do next. Mangara believed himself to hold the magic needed to open it. He did not.

Thesso decided to discuss this situation with Tarkin, so he contacted him. Tarkin responded at once because he too had been feeling uneasy without knowing why. He had never seen or felt the Hunti. But today he would see, firsthand, the extent of their evil. At the end of this day, he would be irrevocably changed. He was with a group of young men who were cleaning fish together at the oceans edge. They had been in a larger group with the women but now they had gone on a shell hunting mission. Kalae was with these women. He reacted to Thesso's contact at once, tossing his head to clear any other distractions from his mind. He walked down the beach away from the others a little. He now felt a sharp sense of urgency followed by one of imminent danger. After Thesso urgent transferring of all the information on the Hunti to Tarkin they, there and then, made a hasty, and very reluctant, decision to close the Portal once again. Thesso would again hide the Portal at the bottom of the ocean. This was a difficult decision to make, but Tarkin had already learned so much and this knowledge along with the information Thesso was sending him, gave him a clear picture of the danger to them all in leaving the Portal open. It was drawing evil like bees to a honey pot.

The situation escalated rapidly and Tarkin, who had already walked along the shore a little way to concentrate better, began running in the direction of his home and the retrieval of the Chest and the disc. He opened his mind to all the information he was being given; weird shapes and images filled him with dread; feelings of fear sickened his gut. His legs felt too weak to support his desire to flee. Finally, he settled enough to listen and absorb what he needed to know. Thesso now fully opened his mind and allowed Tarkin to experience the Hunti, to feel their evil energy and then he showed him the mind picture of them and various other hideous creatures flooding the village, his home. This information, though necessary, was terrifying and once more he fought for release from his paralysing fear.

Thesso continuously calmed him and told him to bring the chest to him at once, to waste no time, he, himself, would come as close to the shore as possible to facilitate the hand over and to offer what protection he could to the fleeing villagers.

As he began running towards the village Tarkin tried to shout out to his companions to warn them and to inform them as to what was going on, but it had proved impossible in his haste and the lack of understanding in the group, so he just screamed for them to run, to find as many of the villagers that they could and go as far out to sea as they could. He asked them to find the women and to tell Kalae that he had said she must go with them without any questions. There was no time for hesitancy. He told them not to fear the great sea dragon if they saw him and that they should trust him. They were bewildered and confused but they saw in his eyes he was deadly serious, so they ran, as fast as they could, to do his bidding.

Tarkin moved swiftly and with purpose, while Thesso maintained mental communication to encourage him and provide prompt warnings. It was now clear the Hunti had reached the homes within the village. Thesso impressed on Tarkin the need to get to the Chest before the Hunti found it. Fortunately for Tarkin the Hunti could not resist feeding on the energies caused by the killing and maiming they caused around them as they went. They were gaining power but were being slowed down as well. They were unaware of the fact that the Disc and thus the Portal was in a Chest with the mind locks. They simple sensed the Portal. Thesso imagined their rage, if they reached the Chest, they would quickly realise they could not open it, and this would send them into a frenzy of hate. He conveyed this to Tarkin. Thesso ran with him via their mind contact and gave him images to save time explaining. Thesso filled Tarkin's mind with an image of Kalae and her friends who were searching for shells along the ocean shore. Tarkin realised his friends would not find her to tell her to stay out to sea as he clearly saw that she and her friends had sailed around the bay this morning to collect shells from a favourite spot where the very best, empty shells were washed ashore by the tide. The image showed they had already found an ample collection so he knew they would return soon. Thesso told Tarkin he would intervene to ensure her safety if he could, but their first mission had to be to get the chest to safety. The images of Kalae spurred his feet, and he ran faster. He was running directly into the Hunti as they wreaked havoc on the villagers.

Soon he had slowed down so as not to be caught, he crept, ran, and where necessary, crawled on his hands and knees, through the village. Tarkin tried to stay calm, he had to reach his own home where the Chest was hidden, and he desperately wanted to find his parents. He hoped he could get to them in time. His fear and panic would attract the Hunti so he mentally talked to himself telling himself all the reasons he could not fail. He had to get to the Chest. As he rounded the corner leading to his home he froze. shock sending ice through his veins. The scene before him was one of nightmares. He was stunned; he could not make any sense of what he was seeing. There were bodies and bits and pieces of bodies strewn out before him. He was unable to look away, the people he knew and loved, were mutilated, they seemed to have been scratched to pieces. He wanted to scream but his heart and his voice had frozen in fear. He felt as if he was paralysed, unable to move, and yet at the same time he was fighting the urge to turn and run away. Thesso was continually trying to calm him and reconnect to his mind. Eventually he reached Tarkin's terrified mind and began to get through to him. Thesso told him that he needed to regain control of himself and calm down otherwise he was likely to become the next victim. 'Get the Chest and come to me,' Thesso repeated over and over like a mantra. Eventually Tarkin's mind responded, and he moved. He made his way slowly and quietly into his home. He had to try to be calm. Focussed. He opened the wooden door and found his parents together on the floor, their heads smashed and their brains spilling out on the floor. Vomit rose in his mouth, but he managed to fight the urge to be sick, he wanted to fall on his knees and gather his Mum and Dad, but there was no time. Tears rolled unchecked down his cheeks. Thesso fed him images of an alive and smiling Kalae and told him he had to get the Chest and get out to protect her. The thought of her being butchered by the Hunti and their accomplices staggered him with its intensity, and he began to see and to concentrate on what he had to do.

Tarkin quietly ran to the corner cupboard, he knelt and removed the bottom drawer, he lifted a flap in the carpet revealing a small chamber. Reaching deep into the chamber he removed the Chest from its hiding place and stuck it under his coat. The Chest was vibrating in his arms, but he held it tightly, then he forced himself to turn away from his home and the bodies of his beloved parents, he knew he could not help them now. Thesso once again urged him to hurry. 'Come to me and then we will get to the boats, we will find Kalae. The Hunti cannot gain access to the Chest, or you once you reach me.' Tarkin closed his eyes to the devastation around him, he tried to shut his ears to the cries of pain and the maniacal laughter filling the village. His movements and the change in position of the Portal had attracted the Hunti and they headed his way in numbers, destroying each other in their excitement, he had to move faster while staying as invisible as he could. Thesso provided him with a mind image of the best pathway to get to the horses, at the same time urging him to waste no time riding to the shore.

His horse came running up to him, but she was uneasy and jumpy, she was pleased to see him, but she was also panicked. He managed to mount her, he did not need, or have time for, any saddle or reins, and he was barely on board when he grabbed her mane tightly, and they reached full gallop as they fled toward the beach. Stealth was no longer an option for them as the noise of him and the horse, along with the calling of the Portal was already bringing every Hunti within miles to their pursuit.

It became obvious to Tarkin and to Thesso that Tarkin did not have enough time to reach him on the beach before the Hunti would overwhelm him. They both urgently sought another way. It is difficult to know what and where and which path to take when your pursuers are almost invisible and only the blood and dirt, they had attracted to themselves in their hunting spree, gave you any idea of their number or where they were. here were hundreds now, the battle having fed them well. Thesso formulated a new plan, and he showed it to Tarkin, he revealed a clear image and a pathway up the mountain, which loomed in front of them on the edge of the sand. The volcano at its peak was the main aim, it would be a perfect place to dispose of the Portal. Tarkin knew what to do and he was quick to direct his mount on the course up the mountain. Tarkin rode hard, fear drove him, as he got farther away from the village his courage returned along with his determination. He knew he rode for his life and for the lives of his neighbours and friends in the village, his heart called out for Kalae, she, and everyone he knew and loved depended on him getting away.

He gave his horse her head relying now on the love and trust that they had shared for all their lives. He knew the mare would keep her feet; she had earned this trust over the years of their partnership. The speed and the terrain were treacherous, but he dared not slow down, the horse sensed this and galloped up the track with all the speed she could muster. Sweat ran down both their backs, but it went unheeded, fear caused adrenaline to course through their veins. Trees and branches tried to whip them from track as they flew by the two were one as they raced up the side of the mountain, getting closer to the volcanic ash at the top. Shale flew up and crashed behind them, but the horse was steady on her feet and her hooves struck the ground with furious intent. They could hear their pursuers below and behind, but fate was on their side and the top was in sight.

The mountain sensed their fear and cried out, red flames belched up and rivers of lava began to pour down the mountain side. Right on cue the volcano was erupting. Great news for the protection of the chest and its precious contents.

When it became clear that the horse could go no further up the mountain because the ground underfoot was now soft and powdery, and rivers of red lava trickled toward them, Tarkin pulled her to a halt. Leaping from the mare's back Tarkin plunged forward, lurching on his feet, his own safety was now of no importance, if he were able to fling the Chest down into the volcano it would not matter what became of him. Breathing heavily, he threw the chest with all his might. The Chest glistened red in the light of the volcanic fire beneath it and beams of light fell across Tarkin, and on the dragon scale he wore on a thong around his neck. Tarkin wrapped his hand around the scale and prayed for himself and those he was protecting. He felt energy surge through him, and he raced back to the horse, which was impatiently waiting for his return, and without hesitation he sprang aboard.

The horse needed no urging to begin the descent down the mountain, away from the fire, rocks, and lava, but into the path of the pursuing Hunti. There would be no mercy when they knew they had failed to obtain the Chest and as he rode, he began to feel their hatred and rage intensify as they perceived the Portal, and therefore its power was lost to them once more.

Tiring fast Tarkin tried to keep up his furious pace, despite his efforts he knew he could not last for much longer. He began to sway, and it was the horse that changed its pace to keep him in the saddle. The horse was becoming increasingly distressed now as the Hunti surrounded them. He felt all was lost and he would not survive the treacherous descent. He did not know if Kalae lived or if she had been killed. There seemed little reason to continue. He knew if they stopped, he and his horse, who had served him all the way up, and now down the mountain and had spared nothing in giving her best, were surely lost. He knew that if they could reach the beach and Thesso, they would be safe, but it seemed an impossible task. He grabbed at the scale around his neck, holding it for courage, he felt its smooth edges and the sharp sides, he felt them cutting into his flesh. Strangely now he felt as if he was drowning. Water wrapped around him and around the horse, the water was soft and sensuous, he relaxed into the soothing feeling and his consciousness left him.

The, now irrevocable, loss of the Portal threw the Hunti into a terrible frenzy, and they turned on each other to assuage the boiling rage and frustration that they were feeling. As they filled themselves, they again pursued Tarkin with vigour and desperation.

RESCUED BY
A DRAGON

Watching anxiously from the shore and experiencing every one of Tarkin's emotions along with him, Thesso felt Tarkin's deep despair, and he could clearly see that Tarkin could not beat the flying Hunti down the mountain side. Suddenly he knew he could not let Tarkin die. He had to do something and do it now! He gathered his own energy and that of the ocean itself. A terrifying storm arose, and it picked up the sea into one huge wave and caused it to rise upward and cover the shore. It rose high up the mountain. A powerful surge of foam and froth rushed upwards, pushed forward by tonnes of water. Smashing everything in its path it picked up Tarkin and his horse and flung them wildly into the air and far out into the ocean. As the water returned to the ocean it dragged huge rocks and trees along with it. Tarkin and the mare had been thrown far enough out to sea to avoid the debris swirling in the water. Thesso plucked Tarkin, from the ocean and set him up upon his large head. Even now he did not rest but began scanning the ocean for the boats that Kalae and her friends had been in earlier in the day.

He knew the small crafts would have been severely buffeted by the huge wave he had caused to save Tarkin. He hoped there was still time to save them all. He wanted to achieve this for Tarkin's sake. Eventually he saw a small craft bobbing in the waves and he headed in its direction. Thesso was fully aware of his own size but because of Tarkin unconscious on his head he could not submerge, he had to stay high out of the water, this added to his fearsome appearance. He knew he would be a terrifying sight for the humans. He would have to save them despite their best efforts to not be saved by a massive fierce looking dragon.

Trying to appear as small as he could Thesso stayed as low as he could. He glided silently and quickly to the first boat. The men who Tarkin had been fishing on the beach with earlier were all in this craft. Along with them were all the people from Ainslia, who they had been able to save, both men, women, and children, so the boat was full of scared and tired people. They all reacted with terror when they saw the huge beast fully breach the surface. Thesso knew there was nothing he could do to allay their fears, so he moved his body around the craft and thus provided calm waters to protect the boat. As the boat steadied, they were able to sit down and focus fully on the terror around them, especially that of being captured by a dragon and the prospect of now being eaten.

Thesso gently moved the boat out to sea where the water was calmer and then dropped into the depths of the ocean. Tarkin still on his head did not awaken but submerged with the dragon. The people began to react as they finally realised, they had been saved, not captured. They started laughing, crying, and talking excitedly all at once, asking themselves how this had happened. The young people had done as Tarkin had asked and had fetched the villagers that were unharmed and had escorted them out to sea. Their happiness at being safe and not being eaten by the sea monster was short lived as they began to worry about other problems. They were aware that their village had been under attack, but they had no idea what had taken place or why. They had been attacked and terrified by an enemy that they could not see nor do any harm to, but it was intent on killing or in fact having them kill each other because of its effect. It had been impossible to fight this enemy and for this reason alone they had gathered all they could and followed the youths to do Tarkin's bidding.

Thesso found Kalae and her girlfriends still clinging to their rolling craft. It was made of bamboo and thus was exceptionally light, it stayed high in the water and rode the waves well. It was, however. tossing and turning like a corkscrew and all they could do was cling to the sides with all their strength.

Thesso preformed the same manoeuvre he had with the villager's boat and brought the small craft out to where the other survivors were finally becoming calmer. This time he kept his huge body above the surface forming a safe harbour for them. How delighted they were to see each other, and they hastily tied the two crafts together.

Thesso began to speak to Tarkin's mind now to wake him. He needed him to communicate with the humans. When he opened his eyes, Tarkin nearly fell into the water in his surprize and hurry to get to his feet. He had no idea where he was or how he had got there. Thesso calmed him and turned his body to show the small boats to Tarkin, who on seeing Kalae launched himself into the water making Thesso's effort to keep him out of the water pointless. He swam to the boats and strong arms eagerly reached out to grab him and pull him aboard. After hugging, crying, and laughing, he told them what had happened.

He told them of the death and mutilation of their families, of the livestock, of his wild ride up the mountain to dispose of the Chest as it was this the Hunti were seeking. He tried to explain why the Hunti were so intent on the Chest, and to tell them of the Portal it contained. He told them it was this Portal that the Hunti desired as they could sense the Portal inside the Chest. To them it made little sense, so he told them of his ride down the side of the erupting volcano, and of how Thesso had saved him by commanding the sea to retrieve him and his horse. He tried to describe the connection he had to the dragon and to explain why the Hunti wanted the Chest. This was not easy. Everyone was in a state of confusion and grief, and they were unable to understand his story. He cried over his guilt and shame for his part in bringing the Hunti to their village and asked them for their forgiveness.

Hours crept passed as the group alternatively wept, grieved, slept, and held each other tightly. Time calmed them and they began to become more accepting of their situation. Thesso pointed out to the villagers that night was now upon them, and they would need food and shelter before it was too cold. He guided them, by commanding a strong breeze, to another island, far away from the Hunti. That night the sea provided an offering of fish for their meal, and they set about the familiar and therefore soothing task of cooking and creating shelters for the night. The strange and unnatural storm still raged between the islands. The wide shore and tall palms on the island provided protection and materials for their shelters. They all worked to help each other, they did not talk about their loss or what had happened to them, but they were all still shocked by the traumatic events of the day.

Later that evening Tarkin took Kalae to the shelter he had built for them. It was their wedding night but there had been no ceremony. It seemed to him that life was unpredictable and waiting any longer to consummate their love would serve no purpose. He took her in his arms and kissed her. Kalae responded with a passion that revealed she felt the same way. They could have lost each other this day. She held him tight and pressed her body to his. Stepping away from each other they began to undress, now naked they laid down together in the primitive, but effective, shelter Tarkin had woven for them. He held her close to him and she did not draw away instead she encouraged him to make love to her. After a long time, they were exhausted, but content and she stayed in his arms and drifted off to sleep Tarkin thanked the Gods for her safety and for the fact that she had not seen any of the atrocities in the village. He did not care about tradition and their missed wedding day. He understood that she would grieve for her wedding day but now was not the time. Their families were gone, and their lives were not the same. Someday they would have a day of celebration. He held her tightly and she slept in his arms. He lay awake reliving the day and he fought the visions of death and mayhem in his head.

When Tarkin awoke the next morning, he sought out Thesso. He was not far away. He was resting in the shallows near to the shore. He sensed Tarkin's approach and went to meet him. Tarkin wanted to know how it was possible he was still alive, and he wanted to thank Thesso for saving him and for protecting his friends as well. He also wanted to know how long they would be safe where they were. He was happy that he had been able to get the Chest to the volcano, but he needed confirmation that he had safely disposed of it into the heart of the fire. He thought he had. This first conversation with Thesso was a difficult one. Tarkin asked if the Chest had been able to stand the heat of the volcano. Thesso informed him that all was well, it was still intact, and the Portal was not accessible without them working together as they had planned, all was as they had hoped.

Even more astounding and hard to understand, Tarkin learnt that in his rescue a powerful transmutation has taken place. To give Tarkin the strength to survive the Hunti's' final attack at the top of the volcano, Thesso has melded himself and Tarkin as one being. This joining also made it possible for Tarkin to withstand the power of the immense storm that gave energy to the sea as it climbed the mountain to rescue him. Tarkin may still appear human, but he was now a dragon, his blood was the blood of a dragon. While Thesso lived Tarkin lived and while Tarkin lived Thesso lived, their lives were irrevocably intertwined. Tarkin would have to learn to control the dragon side of himself, but Thesso was there to guide and help. Thesso was having no trouble holding the human aspects of himself, but he felt one day they may become of value to him. It was all a bit unbelievable and quite alarming, but Tarkin decided not to dwell on this miracle and to turn his attention to day-to-day happenings. To Kalae, to the plight of the villagers and to making their island home as comfortable as possible. Even as he put his dragon blood to the back of his mind, he was humbly aware of the sacrifice Thesso had made on his behalf, as he was aware that his vulnerability, as a human, made Thesso vulnerable along with him.

Later that day while walking along the beach Tarkin spotted a large animal up ahead of him on the sand. It was quietly eating the short grasses that grew close to the edge of the dunes. He began to run towards the beast as he had recognised it as his horse, the horse hearing him calling out its name, raised her head and whinnied excitedly, she began trotting towards him. He was so excited and happy to see her. He did not think she would have survived the huge wave that washed them both out to sea, but she had and had managed to swim to the shore. He was overwhelmed by his emotion at their reunion. Together they walked back to the others where Tarkin tended to the horse's needs. The villages raced up to greet them, it was a perfect reunion, and all their spirits were lifted.

Thesso and Tarkin decided that it would be necessary to stay, here on the island, where they were taking refuge and not to return to Ainslia at once. They felt it would take time for the Hunti to stop pursuing them, or more correctly hunting for the Chest. Thesso told them that staying on the island was perfect as it was small, and therefore he and Tarkin could protect it together if necessary. He could create storms at sea around the island thus making it impossible for the Hunti to reach the villagers in their safe harbour. The high winds he could call upon, when necessary, would shred the energy fields of the Hunti, and they would be forced to retreat. The villagers agreed and began to set up a more permanent settlement. Tarkin and Thesso returned to Ainslia to save what possessions they could and to collected anything that what could help them to get comfortably established on the island. Every few months Thesso would visit Ainslia personally to see if they would be safe to return, but he would come back every time and ask them to be patient a little longer.

Years passed by and finally there was no sign or evidence of the Hunti staying in the area. If there were any left, they had gone into hiding, Thesso would sense them if they resurfaced. Tarkin and Thesso along with the villagers all agreed that it was time to return to the mainland and they all wished to return to their homeland in Ainslia. As well as providing an escape for the villagers the huge waves and intense winds that Thesso had created to save Tarkin years ago had cleansed Ainslia. The buildings and those who had lost their lives in the battle with the Hunti, had gone to the seabed. An array of structures did remain intact but not everyone's home had survived the sea. Each villager returned to his land and began to rebuild their homes, farms, and their lives. They each worked on their own properties but as they could they helped each other to get reestablished.

Tarkin and Kalae returned to Ainslia with three beautiful children, two fine young boys who looked like their father and a beautiful daughter, who, except for her hair, was the image of her mother. The three children had inherited the dragon blood, but it was an unknown how this would manifest in each of their lives. Karmen was a beautiful child, unlike all the other villagers she had bright, red hair. From an early age her hair seemed to grow over night so at just three years old it was halfway down her back. She was a strong and muscular girl and had a fiery temper. Her brothers, Lase and Eske were often sorry they tried to tease her. The two boys were also strong and muscular, but they did not have Karmen's red hair and thankfully they were calmer in temperament.

Over the years the group settled back into life in Ainslia. Tarkin and Kalae's children grew up and took partners, new babies were born, and the dragon line passed down. The two enjoyed a long happy marriage but the inevitable happened and Kalae grew older and eventually she passed away. Tarkin was deeply saddened by her passing, she had never fully understood his transmutation, yet she had loved and embraced him with her whole heart. After Kalae's death Tarkin was alone for years.

His children and grandchildren prospered, and his family increased in number. Tarkin eventually took a new partner, she knew of his past, but she loved him and was not afraid of the dragon side of him. In this way a new people came into being. For all intents they were human, but the blood of a powerful dragon flowed in their veins. As Tarkin's children grew it was obvious that not all had the same powers, the male line produced male and females with strong skill sets. A match for Tarkin, but they did not have the connection to Thesso that he held. This was great because their lives were not connected with his. The female line produced a different skill set, this lineage did not have the dragon powers of physical strength, but they possessed deep intuitive powers, healing was one such skill, and many people sought their aid over the years. The maternal line had the power of compulsion which is extremely rare in any species, and others were shape changers. Although the skills sets were different this was most definitely not an ordinary family of humans. Not everyone had the gift of longevity. As in every family jealousy arose as the children were put out by their difference. Tarkin spent a good deal of his time talking with all his children and attempting to maintain a peaceful family life.

Tarkin himself remained strong and he did not appear age at all. He had over time discovered that other attributes of being a dragon were now his, but he still did not understand them all, he still had more to learn after all this time. One of these attributes was the ability to summons fire at will. The majority of the Dragon People had the same skills as their father did. Creating fire when you needed it was a useful trait especially around the house, in the workshops and while camping out or hunting. Tarkin became adept at using the fire when necessary but also not letting too many people know that he had this ability. Enhanced senses were now part of his everyday experience, and he could feel the energies, and changes in the weather from afar and long before anything happened. He could hear the lightest sound and see for long distances. He and his descendants could communicate with each other and with all dragons without speaking aloud. They had this connection with other species in the same manner. Thesso had manipulated weather and tides to save Tarkin in his desperate attempt to escape the Hunti and the erupting volcano, he told Tarkin that he could do the same, but Tarkin had not yet tried this. He was always conscious of not being too different and of protecting his family.

PART TWO

AN EPIC JOURNEY

A small party of dwarves marched west, away from their home city of Christiana in the eastern parts of Pardow. Their destination, a mythical cavern, where it was said three dragons were being held captive. Legend has it they were to be found beneath the city of Cam, far to the west. The dwarves sought the dragons for they needed their wisdom and knowledge as they needed help in deciphering a riddle. This riddle was contained in the drawings etched on the side of a small Chest. They hoped the answer to the riddle and the drawings would allow them to open this mysterious Chest. Their King, King Paelion had sent them on this journey which he considered of utmost importance to their people. He had chosen his best warriors, and his best intuits. The King believed finding the dragons would answer all of their questions. A sizeable portion of the journey would have to be made on the surface, and it is well known that a dwarf is most comfortable underground. Unfortunately, there was no choice as they were being driven by the urgency of the quest. They had to do whatever was necessary, so they would have to march, crawl, run or dig, to the city of Cam.

THE DRAGONS
OF CAM

The legend of the Dragons of Cam was common throughout Pardow because King Elgrade promoted the idea vigorously. Over one hundred and fifty years ago King Elgrade of Cam had lured a family of three dragons to his kingdom with a promise of peace to all dragons if they came and lived within the city walls. A very good deal for the King as no one would dare question him or attack him when dragons were at his side and it was also good for the dragons as it provided a haven, not only for Josepheos, Shari, his life partner, and their daughter Miriam, but it was a truce with all dragons.

For years all was peaceful and dragons were creatures of honour and treated with great love and respect in the kingdom, but the King became old and listened to those who hated dragons and feared them more. There were black hearted men in the city who hated the dragon's ability to know them as they were, and not what they projected on the outside. It was impossible to do anything of evil intent as the dragon's always alerted the King before you could hardly have formed the thought. This peace within the kingdom was destroyed as old King Elgrade, in the frailty of age, was no match for these cunning and evil people and allowed himself to be convinced to get rid of the dragons. He became increasingly fearful of their power, due to the lies he was presented with daily, and decided to lock the three dragons away. He knew that trying to kill them would be extremely unwise as that would bring the wrath of all other dragons upon him and Cam. He did not want to be responsible for changes in the energy of the earth and spiritual realms either, who knew what the result of that would be.

The huge cavern that had already been hewn out of the rocks beneath the city for their respite now became a prison for the dragons and for the servants that took care of them. No servant that went down into the caverns every came out, dead or alive. Food and supplies were sent to the cavern via a series of complicated winches. Wastes were removed in the same way. Daylight entered the cavern via a series of mirrors that reflected the light until it reached the depths of the cave. The outer sunlight also entered the cavern this way. As a new King came and went, they kept the status quo and the dragons remained in their gilded cage, a beautiful prison but a prison, nonetheless. The walls of this cavern were lined with diamonds as the King was extremely wealthy and he knew that dragons loved diamonds, this was in one way an appeasement to their capture, but it also made it impossible for them to communicate, mind to mind with other dragons. A sad loss for the Dragons.

As the dwarfs began their perilous journey to find them, the three dragons, were enjoying a rest, they yawned and stretched out their wings in their prison home. They were very much aware of the situation that King Elgrade the First, had put them in. They knew he had done it out of fear. Once the old King Elgrade had both admired and respected them, he was in awe of their vast knowledge, magical powers, and their physical capabilities. As he grew older, he had fallen victim to the suggestions of evil and ambitious members of his own court, they had begun to spin tales and confusion as to the dragons' loyalty and their intentions. His aging mind, and the prompting of these scheming souls, caused him to believe that the dragons would harm him and his people.

The King did not want to kill the dragons because he feared their deaths as much as their lives. A dragon by its very essence must be honest and true, it cannot maintain its connection with the universal consciousness, the one, if it is not. A dragon therefore hates nothing and has no malice, to kill one would be an act of great treachery. The King was also quick to acknowledge that a kingdom with three huge dragons in its artillery, held great power and influence across the earth.

He kept them in great splendour, but they had no freedom. They did not venture from their prison which was deep inside the grand cavern that had formed under the city as the underground rivers ran their course to the sea. The city of Cam was built over the vast system of caves, cumulating in this great space. While they had been free to roam the city this cavern was enlarged especially for them, in these times they were free to come and go as they pleased. Now they saw no one, other than the King himself and the servants that were assigned to their care. These servants also lived inside the cave system and were subject to imprisonment themselves as they served the dragons. No one came in and no one came out of the cavern and caves.

The dragons reckoned that they had been in the cavern at least one hundred human years, or more, which did not bother them as time is inconsequential to a dragon and is not measured in lineal years as humans' measure time. Dragons are extremely patient and long suffering; they are powerful both physically and mentally, and they have the amazing ability to commune without speech via a mind transfer or connection. They could not communicate with other dragons outside their prison but as dragons were very stoic, they accepted their position would be resolved when the time was right.

They had considered an escape mission but lack of help from the outside made it far too dangerous. Unnecessary blood would, certainly, be spilt on both sides. To lose his wife or daughter was not a risk Josepheos was prepared to take. Miriam was a teenager in dragon years, but she would be a mature dragon before he knew it. Although he knew patience was called for, and even though they were a very patient species, as the years moved by the he became increasingly concerned as to their plight. Their captivity had not been addressed by the succession of earthly Kings. Despite their regular communication with the new rulers, fear, superstition, and ignorance was being passed down from King to King. There had now been two changes of Monarchs but none of them had altered their situation.

AN UNEXPECTED GUEST

Great excitement buzzed throughout the cavern as suddenly and unexpectedly a stranger was ushered unceremoniously into the cave. Servants ran this way and that, murmuring in excited, but hushed and fearful, voices. Confusion reigned, alongside the excitement in the cavern for a long moment but then relief flooded in as everyone realised their visitor was quite small and appeared harmless, despite the fact he was heavily armed. He had an enormous grin on his face. He did indeed look quite friendly and excited. Finally, everyone, servants, and dragon, alike, simply stared in astonishment at the visitor. The dragons were the first to react and come to grips with what they were seeing.

There, before them, inside the impenetrable Grand Cavern, stood a dwarf. He was short even by the standard of dwarfs. He was about three feet tall, and he appeared, at first observation, to be quite old although he was middle aged. He was dressed in the simple travel clothes of a leather vest and pants. Knee knee-high boots adorned his feet and legs. It was obvious that he was a warrior by the sword at his waist and knives in his belt. On his back was tied an axe and a hammer. He was dressed for a fight with whatever might be encounter along his way. His long hair was tied at his nape, and it was a light gold in colour. His face was wrinkled and his eyebrows long, his ears, pointing skyward had large tufts of yellow hair poking out, his eyes were a deep emerald blue and as he looked up at the dragons, his eyes were filled with excitement and barely contained joy. His demeanour was not that of a frightened prisoner. He danced from foot-to-foot, hopping in the air every now and then, hardly able to contain his own joy at finding himself in the presence of the dragons. He was unafraid and certainly seemed to be enjoying the fuss his arrival was causing. 'What on earth are you doing here?' Miriam, the youngest dragon, asked excitedly. The little dwarf grinned widely and said, 'Well I have hardly had a choice as to my whereabouts since I was captured this morning.'

'Do not be afraid, it is a long time since we last ate a dwarf. Come, sit, and tell us your story,' chorused the dragons, laughing aloud at their joke. 'We can certainly do with the entertainment and indeed you appear eager to tell your story. 'If I am not mistaken, I would say your capture has not upset you at all in fact I think it has worked in your favour.'

The dragons settled into their luxurious nests and Josepheos and Miriam made a comfortable space between their huge bodies, patted it firmly and beckoned the dwarf to sit. They then bid the servants to bring refreshments. Therron the head of the servants sent all the others racing off in all directions. The servants hurried off to do his bidding, eager to return and hear for themselves what was going on. They too were excited and did not want to miss a thing. Therron then found himself a seat near to the dragons, far enough away to be discreet but close enough to hear everything.

Huge trays of all sorts of meat and game and buckets of mead, a variety of fresh berries and other fruits of all colours and sizes, huge and tiny cakes and loaves of bread appeared as if from nowhere. Thornfoot was amazed, but he learned later that the dragons were not necessarily carnivorous. When possible, they ate a wide and varied diet. Here in the cavern, they were never hungry and indeed were given the best of everything to eat and drink and to ensure their health and wellbeing. The King did not feel comfortable or safe with these three dragons roaming around his city but while they were his 'guests' as he liked to call it' living under his feet he treated them with a great deal of caution and respect. The dragons made themselves comfortable, excited, and happy, one hundred years or more with an undisturbed routine made this an exciting interlude to say the least.

'Let me introduce myself,' said the dwarf. 'My name is Thornfoot, I am of the Clan Elan. I am on an errand of utmost importance and urgency. It is not possible to understand just how important, at this point, but I have personally been sent by the Great Dwarf King Elon to find, and to gain an audience with you, the dragons of King Elgrade of Cam.'

The dragons sat up expectantly, Elon had been king of the dwarf clan for over one thousand years, and it pleased them to know he was still alive and that they would have news of him and why he was searching for them. News of the outside world seldom penetrated their prison. They could not understand why the King had allowed the dwarf to be brought to their presence as it was a very strictly obeyed rule that they were not to have any contact or knowledge of the world outside the caverns.

The dragons were knowledgeable in regard to dwarfs, they knew that they lived beneath the surface of the earth, that they were miners and that they had vast kingdoms that where mostly unknown by the humankind that lived on top of the earth. Dwarfs had an uncanny knack of knowing what was on your mind before you voiced anything and they believed strongly in magical powers, especially in the power of jewels, crystals, and stones of the earth. It was rumoured they could control your thoughts and thus your deeds if allowed to gain control of your mind. Dwarfs were fierce warriors and although legend says they loved a good fight, they also loved peace and quiet. They protected their own kind with strength and determination and seldom were put upon because anyone who recognised a dwarf was not interested in a fight with one of them. The dwarfs were also extraordinarily rich if richness is measured by human standards. Their cities were made of gold and decorated with precious stones and jewels. Christiana, Thornfoot's home was no exception to this rule.

What the dwarfs wanted with them and more importantly, how they had been able to find them was extremely interesting to the three dragons. The dragons were keen to know what it was that was of so much concern to the dwarfs, what was so important that they not only ventured to the surface but travelled vast kilometres in human territory to come here to find them. How had they discovered the diamond cavern? How did they even know about the dragons' imprisonment and whereabouts and how did they get into Cam and more puzzling than all of this, how had Thornfoot managed to get into the Grand Cavern? What on earth was going on! Despite wanting to know all of this they held their tongues, remained quiet, and allowed Thornfoot to have the floor.

THORNFOOT
TELLS HIS STORY

Thornfoot told the dragons about the Chest and its drawings and their inability to open it. At the mention of a Chest the dragons became even more attentive and appeared to be alarmed. 'May we see this Chest as soon as possible?' Thornfoot told them the Chest remained under guard in Christiana, as they had not been able to open it, and they had been extremely cautious as to its contents. The dwarf King had decided to not disturb it and set a guard until the dragons had been found and consulted as what it was and what it held. Thornfoot also told them that they did recognise the indestructible metal from which it was constructed. The dragons asked him if he could describe its decorations for them. 'There is no need for that.' said Thornfoot, as he began to remove the small leather vest which he wore over his shirt. Turning it inside out he revealed the finely drawn picture on the inside. Etched in the soft leather was a picture of the dragon and of the Chest. There was no need for Thornfoot to talk to them and describe the drawings on the Chest, it was all there before their eyes.

While waiting patiently to hear Thornfoot's' story of his and his fellow dwarves' journey to find them. The dragons began to feel an immense excitement. Could this be the time that they would be free. They held their emotions to themselves and took the small waistcoat that Thornfoot handed them.

On viewing the intricate and beautiful drawings of the Chest, the two older dragons shouted in unison with great emotion and excitement in their voices. Immediately they restrained their excitement. 'This is a picture of the Great Sea Serpent, Thesso. He is the greatest of the dragons that protect the oceans of the earth. 'He does not look like we do because he is an ocean dweller. Thesso is an ancient dragon of great power and influence. Before we tell you what we know of Thesso we would like you to tell us all the story that led you here to Diamond Cavern and to us.

Thornfoot was aware of their need to know the full story before they trusted him, he was happy to tell them everything he knew, and he felt confident that when they had heard the whole story, they would help him. He accepted their prudence as wise and happily began the story right at the beginning.

The dragons sat back and rested quietly while Thornfoot recounted the story of the dwarf team's journey to Cam, and to find them.

FINDING THE CHEST

'Our story began when we were mining in the southernmost part of our territories. We were right under the volcano that is on the beach at Ainslia. A tunnel had been opened months ago, and we have already mined hundreds of metres into the mountain. As is usual for us we were searching for gold and looking for precious stones. We continued working on a downward spiral, and it was here, deep in the underground we discovered something unusual buried in the rock layers. Something that had not formed naturally. What we had found was rectangular in shape and looked like one of the small chests we carried when travelling, only this one was made of metal, and ours are made of leather or wood. The Chest was deeply embedded into the rocky layers of the rock. We were so deep down that it is uncertain as to who could have buried the object. Usually, we are the only ones down so far, and as the under-surface is well mapped, we were surprised and a little uncertain as to how we should proceed. The discovery was so unusual that we decided to send word to King

Paelion, the leader of our Clan, for advice and instructions before we tried to dig the Chest out of its rocky encasement.

He had no concept of what we had unearthed, and he sent word that he would attend in person. We awaited his arrival with impatience. A guard was set over the Chest, and we all stood around talking and offering suggestions as to what the object was and why it was down here. As chief of the guard unit that was working in the area I stayed with the Chest as others went about their work. I was not sure why, but I was attracted to the Chest and somehow felt it was significant.

The King was obviously excited too because he came in haste, without his usual entourage. His most trusted guardsmen were with him, along with his most senior advisors, however he chose to take only two men with him when he began the descent into the tunnel. His senior advisor Graynor, and the head of his personal guard, Moon Ray, accompanied him into the mine.

King Paelion was a truly magnificent sight, today, without his entourage, he was still impressive. Dwarfs and their families all ran along beside him as he approached the mine, to see what was happening, and to cheer their King. He stood almost 5ft tall, larger than most dwarfs, he was as broad as he was tall. There was not an ounce of fat on him, hard, thick muscle bulked out his frame. His beard, as black as the day it appeared, to the amusement of his parents, was huge and brushed to a sheen, it was adorned here and there with gemstones and bells and gold pieces moulded into shapes. His eyebrows met in the middle and formed a hood over his emerald, green eyes that now glistened with excitement. His nose was long and straight, his lips were full, with a wide generous mouth. He was smiling today which gave his appearance a happy glow. He wore jewels and decorations anywhere one could fit. Gold rings studded with precious stones hung from his ears and eyebrows. His hair was plaited and banded in leather; today he wore no crown, and no decorations adorned his brow, he wore only a sensible tunic and breeches. He was prepared for a journey deep into the earth.

Excitedly he began his descent underground, deep into the cool moist air of the underworld, over one hundred metres below lay something new and unknown, a thrill of excitement flowed through his mind and the accompanying adrenalin made his climb easy.

He made the downward spiralling journey quite speedily, despite his size and age. As soon as I saw he had arrived, I beckoned him to the area where I was standing guard over the Chest. He examined the Chest for a long time, systematically inspecting it and carefully removing the surrounding soil. He then gave the order for us to continue our excavation of the mystery object.

The first team of diggers came quickly descending the tunnel speedily and set about the excavation with great enthusiasm and with immense excitement and a little trepidation thrown in. Around about thirty more dwarfs arrived and joined the dig, they worked in shifts of just minutes to keep their digging speed up to the maximum. They quickly had the Chest unearthed and on full display.

What lay before us was a metal box, not large by any means but one which, for all its lack of size was at once impressive. It was a beautifully carved piece with elaborate drawings and designs, which centred upon a fierce looking dragon-like creature. We decided that it was indeed a Chest and had been made to carry something extraordinary if the exterior decorations said anything at all. The Chest also had a heavy metal band that sealed it and a large locking device, which was made of gold or brass, held the seal tightly in place. There was a keyhole, but no key revealed itself anywhere in the vicinity.

The King deliberated with his advisor, and it was decided to open the Chest right here where it was. Everyone was excited to open the Chest so he decided not to wait, more importantly, he did not want to return to his castle bringing with him the Chest which may hold something of ill import or be dangerous to his citizens. If it held something supernatural or explosive, then best to keep it here in the deep, deep belly of the earth.

There was also the chance that the Chest was empty, and it would be very embarrassing to have made such a fuss for nothing. Overall, it seemed not only prudent but also wise to open the Chest where it was. Despite the Kings interest being extremely high he followed the advice of Graynor, his advisor and went with Moon Ray back up away from the tunnels and to the surface in a huge cavern which was part of the underground city of Christiana. Everyone except for myself, and the King's advisor, was commanded to leave the area, not only to leave the tunnel, but to climb up to the cavern, away from any danger.

When the area was cleared, Graynor, and I began with great excitement and expectation to open the Chest. To our dismay and frustration nothing we could do would open the lock. We could not open or break the lock and none of the tools we had would pierce the seal.

Despite sending for everything we could think of and everyone who may have an idea to help us we had to admit defeat. The Chest was transported from the mine to the castle, where it was placed in a secure chamber under guard until a method for opening it could be determined.

The Chest was about 30cms long and quite narrow about 15cm wide and the same in depth. Whatever it held could not be large, at least not on a physical measure that is. The Chest was made of metal but not one we recognised. On the outside of the Chest was an engraving of an unusual dragon. A group of Elders had heard of a sea serpent that had fought with the Humans centuries ago, but they had little knowledge that was helpful. We were certain it did not look like any dragon we had encountered. The historians and recorders were called in, but none had anything positive to help identify the flight-less dragon. We had no earlier recordings of such a being in the history of our city. He was long and thin, his head was that of a dragon but his body more like a serpent, he had wings, but they were small and could not have been for flying.

I fear we had no idea what beast this was, but we knew we would have to find out, as it was clear to us that this knowledge would be the key to opening the Chest. We were now totally intrigued with the Chest and could not wait to find out its secrets.

A team of specialist artisans began to meticulously copy the drawings. On one side of the Chest the scene was of majestic mountains dominated by a central peak that towered high above the others. The top of the mountain was surrounded by clouds but on second look we could see it was wreathed by smoke that billowed out of the peak. The ocean licked the feet of the mountains and trees grew right to the edge of the water. Here and there the image was inlaid with precious stones which the dwarfs had also copied for authenticity.

The beautifully etched scene on the lid was dominated by the large dragon-like creature rising out of the water. He was standing on his tail as he reared upward. His head was large and thrown back, his eyes gleamed, his teeth, glinting in the sun, were large and appeared sharp. His posture strong and aggressive. Fire flared from his mouth. This scene portrayed a sense of power and energy. It was difficult to look at anything else.

On the sea below the dragon was a small wooden craft. In the craft was a young man. In comparison to the huge beast above him he was tiny, but it was possible to see he was human, young, hand-some, and comfortable in the situation. His arms reached upward toward the dragon, and he held a tiny disc in his hand. The disc was inlaid with tiny specks of rainbow-coloured jewels. He appeared to be either giving the disc to the dragon or receiving it from him. It was not possible to tell. There was a definite, tangible connection between the two.

While the Chest was being copied for historical records and the recorders had been memorising its every detail the King had been discussing with his advisors and warriors as to what they could or should do. He spent days with his counsellors, wise men, and senior advisors along with the chief of his war counsel and his spiritualists and dreamers to consider the best course of action to take.

They looked at the new situation from all angles, the best one was to simply rebury the box and move on to a different mine tunnel or keep it in their own care until such time as a solution arose. But dwarfs are curious and stubborn, among other things, and none of these ideas was acceptable. Finally, they all agreed on one thing, the huge dragon pictured in such fearsome splendour on the Chest had the key or knew the key to unlocking both the Chest and its secrets, either him or the human. Finally, they decided to return the Chest in the shaft where it was found. A guard was placed over the Chest night and day and would remain so until a clue to its contents could be found.

King Paelion, having no other ideas on what to do about opening the Chest, decided that locating the legendary Dragons of Cam would be the best step forward. We had heard of your imprisonment, and as we were aware that Dragons are rare in this land and time, we decided that the legend of the dragons of Cam was more than likely to be true. We decided to look for you in Cam. King Paelion felt it was the only chance of success, in gaining knowledge of the Chest, and the identity of the dragon pictured on it. He hoped with this knowledge the question of what the Chest held and indeed how to open it, would be answered. He knew a dragon's memories last forever and that when a dragon feels death is upon him the last action, he takes is to pass his own memories to one of his kin. The memories and knowledge are passed from generation to generation therefore nothing, once experienced and learned, is ever lost.

The King understood that to find one man in the sea of humanity above them seemed an unsurmountable task. The lives of men were short, so it was unlikely this man still lived to be found in any case. Finding a dragon, even an ordinary one, if one can ever call a dragon ordinary, however, may be possible.'

'The Dwarf King knew that it would be difficult to get to the city of Cam and to find the dragons, but he also understood that gaining an audience with them would be much harder. One thing however was in our favour and that was the fact the cavern was underground, and underground is the territory of the dwarves. If anyone or anything could get in, we could.

How to get to the city and access the dragons was the subject of a long, noisy, and excited debate that lasted for days. How does a team of dwarfs, that are happier underground and rarely poke their heads above the surface, get to Cam, a surface city of humans, and having arrived there, how do they get into the caverns, that for over hundreds of years have been sealed off and heavily guarded?'

THE TEAM

Finally, it was decided a small group, acting with stealth, may have the best hope of success. They did not believe King Elgrade would allow an emissary to see the dragons and indeed he could, and would, demand the Chest for himself. Wars had been fought over lesser things. A war with Cam was not what we wanted but we also were not going to hand over something we did not understand, a possible weapon, to our past enemy.

Nine of us were chosen to take the perilous journey to the City of Cam. I was chosen to lead this group. The other members were, Hegel an Elder like me with a long pedigree of fearsome fighting and an astute strategist. Elzer was chosen for his keen mind and ability to see vast distances. He was also very experienced with a bow. Elkfast, chosen for speed as a runner and a thinker, Treeturn has a wonderful knowledge of trees and plants and their uses, and be brought the ability to communicate with the plants and animals to the team. Dwaymoon was chosen for his skill as a chemist, he knew the power of herbs and metals, what to eat and what not and what may be used to further the cause whichever way was needed. If we needed explosives when we got to the caverns, he would find the right compound to provide this.

Myrtle was one of three females to take the journey, she was a skilled bowman and a recorder of events, she never forgets what she has seen or experienced. The second female in the team, Frurose's skill was in healing, she was with us to keep us all healthy and to aid us in case of injury or wounding. Frurose was also a shape shifter and was able to move outside of her body if necessary and to take on the form of other creatures. Pria was the smallest dwarf and the youngest, she could run like the wind and was fearsome in battle, but her true skill was persuasion, or compulsion. There were very few living beings that could resist a direct request from Pria.

Our preparations began at once. Artisans began the intricate process of copying the images onto the vest for me to wear. While this painstaking work was going on we all worked on our fitness and battle skills. We had moved into a garrison together so that we could become better acquainted with each other and learn all the individual talents and skills we brought to the group. We got to know each other as we spent the days training and the evenings, we planned how to use our unique skills for our quest. This time spent together gave us a better understanding as to why we had been chosen for the mission.

It was during this time I noticed Dwaymoon was attracted to Pria, he became a little nervous in her direct company, she seemed happy to have his attention, but I did not see any romantic interaction between them. I did not want her distracted or compromised but I did understand matters of the heart as well. I decided to keep my observations to myself and while any relationship between them did not interfere with our mission I would keep silent. Pria's skills were necessary for our success, only a few dwarves, or any creature, had the abilities of compulsion that she possessed in abundance. I had a feeling that this unique ability would come to our advantage down the track.

The cartographers worked with the recorders and historians to draw a surface map for the area between Christiana and Cam and any towns and cities we may come across on the way. Rivers and lakes, mountains and seas stood between us and the dragons. These held no fear for us, as we meet all these natural wonders below the ground, but we understood more of the underworld, and we knew there were countless unknown factors on the surface. A map was also produced of the underground paths that may be useful to us, we would travel faster underground, and we would need respite from the dry surface air and the rays of the sun.

There was one known dwarf city along our way, a distant arm of Clan Elan. The city of Joannamere was the subjects of childhood legends. We were eager to see the city and meet our clansmen. We were, indeed, embarking on a remarkable journey.

Our first challenge was the surface and the daylight. Overall, we had limited experience above the ground, and we were extremely excited but also terrified at the prospect. I had spent time above the ground, as had Hegel, but it had been years ago, and we all needed the preparation time for this journey. Treeturn was the only one of us who had spent considerable time above ground as he studied the plants and herbs, but none of the rest of us had current experience.

The suns were perceived to be our first major, enemy, and to know we would be in their direct light was scary. There was also the heat of the day and the thinness of the air above ground, there would be little to no moisture in the air to protect our lungs from the suns either, there was no way to guess how long the quest would take and how long before we returned. We would simply set off and put one foot in front of the next, face each challenge as it presented itself. If necessary to get out of the sunlight we would find one of the underground paths or dig into the earth as needed for respite.

When all the organisation was complete, and it was time to get on our way we all took time to spend with our families and friends. I hugged my beautiful wife, Therese; thirty years we had been together, and she always looked the same to me. I felt like a very young man in the first throes of love when I held her and assured her that this task was like all the others, and in many ways, it was better as there was no known threat and it was unlikely that there would be any fighting along the way. She shook her head and said, 'there usually is with you, but I do hope you are right this time. You are not getting any younger my love.' At this I picked her up twirled her in the air and gave her a last long kiss, I set her down, picked up my bag and I walked quickly out the door.'

'We began our journey to the surface slowly and careful, taking more rest stops as we neared the surface, in preparation for stepping out of our underground world and into the sun and the beginning of the greatest adventure of our lives. We spent our time discussing and pondering ways and means to travel unseen in human territory, of finding our way to Cam and how to get access to the dragons.'

STEPPING INTO
THE LIGHT

ᵀFinally, we stepped out into the light of the outer sun, which
was particularly close to Pardow tonight, it was as bright as
daylight but not as harsh, we had waited just below the surface for
some time while the first sun went down, taking turns to peer out. I
experienced a feeling of excitement and expectation and a good deal
of delight. We were on the surface, and so far, we had not dissolved
and nothing bad had occurred. It was incredibly beautiful above the
surface; we could see stars that were just forming in the sky. The
sky itself was immense and made us feel very tiny in comparison, a
million different things impacted on our senses, visuals and smells,
sound and feeling came at us so fast we were a little overwhelmed. We
only stayed outside on the surface for a brief time and then returned
underground to digest what we had learned and felt, we would then
store all this information for when we may need it. We all agreed that
being completely exposed to the surface world was both, daunting
and exciting. At the same time.

'We had decided to stay on the surface for as little time as was necessary throughout the journey but unfortunately the very first part of our trek northwards required that very thing. We must stay on the surface. For strategic reasons our home, the underground city of Christiana had been built against a wall of granite rock, at least two miles thick, which protected us on one side and there was a large underground sea to protect us on the other. These natural barriers provided an impenetrable defence. There was a time when the dwarf clans were at war, this was centuries before our time, but we had never been allowed to forget. We could not pass through, or under, the sea, so we had no choice but to trek around the rock, we would have to stay on the surface for a considerable length of time.

'Once we had acclimatised with being out in the sunlight, we decided to make our way through the centre of the Enchanted Forest or Den Dargo as it was historically known. We set up camp and rested for the first night and then early next morning we entered the forest. The shade of the trees would provide us cover from the sun and the air was soft and moist, as it was underground. Travelling through the centre of the woods would also shorten our journey. There were tangled masses of trees and mossy bogs, beautiful flowers, and strange wildlife. This forest it was said, was also the home of witches, dryads, woodland nymphs and other esoterically beings.'

'There was also the possibility that other species lived here, as centuries before it was told that people had travelled vast distances across space and time and had stayed here on Pardow, either by choice or catastrophic event. How this occurred we did not know, and we thought it may not be true, but legends do start somewhere so we were careful. We hoped not to meet anything harmful either of this world or any other. We thought they were made up by storytellers to keep children out of the woods. The trees themselves were alive, and watching our every move, or so it seemed. We did not fear the trees however, as they were familiar to us and because we believed in, and trusted Elzar's and Treeturn's ability to ensure us all a safe passage with their unique talents of communicating with the trees and other natural beings that lived in the forest. If anything were planning to attack us, they would know.'

We were more cautious of the humans in the village of Ainslia as the forest was quite near the outskirts of town, and humans often came into the edges of the woods to collect mushrooms and herbs. The girls collected flowers to put in their hair. It had been years since dwarves and humans had mixed and we had no idea of their reaction if they saw us in the forest. Our plan was to stay as close to the centre of the forest and walk straight through. When we came out the other side, we would be able to head down under the earth into the realm of the river dwellers. They were of the Clan of Elan, but they lived on the banks of a great river that ran under the ground and flowed all the way to the eastern oceans, its head was in the Serendipity Sea a thousand miles to the north. Never once did this river break the surface.'

'When we returned underground, we would travel the Dwarf roads and cross the great Lombrox Bridge. It had been built across the river by the dwarf King Lombrox eons past and was the subject of legends and held great fame and respect in the dwarf kingdoms. We had been taught from an early age that we must remove any headwear when even mentioning the name Lombrox, and to keep our eyes downcast. What would be needed from us at the bridge we did not know but first things first, we had to get through the forest.'

THE ENCHANTED FORREST

The forest was clothed in mist and a weak sun tried unsuccessfully to penetrate the heavy fog, the light through the branches flickered and moved, confusing our minds, we saw and felt movement, perhaps it was real, but I am sure a lot that worried us was imagined. Moss hung off low branches giving the appearance of living beings and here and there the branches dipped into the water beneath. Elzar, because of his incredible vision and his connection to the energies, lead the way. On his right Elkfast, who would commune with the plants and trees probed ahead of us. We hoped between them they would be able to project our intentions onto the forest and to all the creatures both physical and spiritual that our intentions were pure and thus to ensure us of a safe passage. If there was anything to avoided ahead of us, we hoped they would sense this, or the plants would tell them where and what to avoid. There was little moving in the forest, but we did see flocks of birds here and there, flitting within patches of sunlight. Their path followed ours for a distance and we felt they were following us but as we could see them, we were not concerned.'

'Humans had been sensed ahead! Elzar raised his hand, and a halt was called. I spotted movement of something larger ahead; a slight feeling of uneasiness came over me. We decided to change our path slightly to go around the humans and whatever it was I had sensed. Suddenly we froze in our tracks as did the humans in front of us. There directly in front of us stood two beautiful young girls, so engrossed and relaxed in their space that they fitted completely into the energies of the forest. We had missed them because of this. We would try to be more careful in future. The girls had been sitting quietly while one of them tied flowers into the other girl's hair.'

'When the realised we were there they appeared shocked, then awestruck and then afraid, all in one moment and their mouths formed to scream. Pria spoke, her voice beautiful and melodious and the screams died in their mouths, their eyes softened, and they began to smile. They both moved towards Pria as if to embrace her, she spoke again and they did just that, laughing and talking as they did so. Happy and relaxed now they led us excitedly to their companions. We had stumbled into a group of young lovers on a picnic. They were happy and not at all afraid of us. Soon we were all talking and laughing, we were offered food, and we enjoyed eating all sorts of delicacies, foods we had never imagined and during all the fun of eating and talking we gathered information from them about the road ahead.'

'We were interested and concerned when they told us of a certain change in the people of the village. Tempers flaring, things going missing and people questioning others behaviour. Accusations were being made, and secretive behaviour was increasing in the village. This was of concern to the group as the villagers were usually quite even tempered and anger was rarely experienced. They had escaped to the woods for peace and quiet and to soak up the relaxing happy energies. They could offer no real explanation for this change in the atmosphere of the village, there was just a niggling feeling that something bad was about to happened and everyone was on edge. After spending an informative hour and having our fill of the strange but tasty food, we reassured the young ones by telling them we would come back this way with any news we learned on our way that may explain this situation and help them.'

None of us made any mention of the mission or the Chest. The young picnickers watched us go and noted this as another strange event in unsettling times.

Our journey through the Enchanted Forrest continued slowly but was not without a variety of interesting occurrences. We had reached a part of the forest which was very thick. The trees grew close, soft creepers had climbed as high as the trees allowed and they now hung in dark columns to the water below. Dark hollows and caves formed within the creepers. If anything were within, we could not see or hear it. The moss was fat and moist. The air was soft on our lungs, and it was quite dark. We did not mind this darkness but finding our way through the mess of roots and marshy grass was difficult. There was, muddy water here and there and we stepped around it as we could. As we stepped over the puddles in our imaginations, they came alive with strange shapes and skinny, slimy, black arms and hands would claw up toward us. If we looked straight at the water, which we did, shouting out in alarm, they disappeared. A glance out of the corner of one's eye revealed them trying their sneaky way of trying to grab on to us. We hurried on in fright our weapons on hand and ready but also keeping to our plan to stay hidden as much as we could and not to draw unnecessary attention to ourselves. The next few days went by without distractions, and we picked our careful path through tangled roots, dappled lights, and broken branches. Sometimes we heard and felt other life forms, but we were not directly accosted, nor did we see anything, imagined or real, we did our utmost to simply ignore it all and keep going.

THE HUNTI
ARE UPON US

We had almost reached the caves that would lead us to the tunnels that would once more take us back to the familiar underground, to the city of Joannamere, and to the reassuring safety of our kin. All of a sudden Elzer raised his hand, and we at once fell silent and motionless. We waited for his instructions.

Elzer was prized for his vision as he could see for over a mile but also, he was connected spiritual to the energies around us, and now I feared this was what had us frozen, waiting. He whispered to us all. 'I have been feeling an increasing sense of urgency for a while now and the presence of a menacing energy, one that has been seeking us out and now I fear it is close upon us. I can only feel the energy and have no vision of this perceived enemy; I will do my best to describe it to you.' He said earnestly, 'it is an angry and urgent feeling, like something is tempting and impelling you to fear it and to run away and at the same time you feel you should stand and defend yourself. It is important to be aware of this menace and to not allow it to penetrate your thoughts to deeply. Do not give into it. Try to show no fear, and do not run for it appears to be growing the more I am conscious of it and as I become afraid it gets stronger. Do not let it feed on our distress as this will cause it to grow stronger. I am sorry I cannot be more specific, but it seems to feed on my emotions.'

Thornfoot paused in his story at this point and looked at the dragons, trying to assess if they were still listening or if he should cut the rest of the story short. They had initially asked for the full story but may be regretting that know. 'Should I continue, or do you want me make this story shorter?' 'Unless there is some urgency in your mind, we would prefer that you tell us everything, it makes it possible for us to learn about all of you and for us to enjoy the story as well, we have not been so entertained for some time,' Josepheos said excitedly. 'Go on if you please."

'Alright it is indeed a long story but hopefully you will all judge me favourably when you have heard it.'

'Now at this point in our story Treeturn called out to the trees asking for protection from the strange energy and asked the trees to hide us where possible, he called on the wind to drive the energies away from us.

I asked the group to join me in a rousing chorus of our national song, and I started to sing loudly, they all stared silently at me as they considered this an unusual request. They then looked to Elzer for his direction as he was the one who had first sensed the enemy. They wanted his reassurance that singing would not incense them further. Elzar understood my request and at his nod they all joined in. As the energies began to swarm over and around us it seemed impossible to hold our ground and not scream and run. With no visible enemy to fight I felt powerless, but I had a loud voice, so I used it and sang even louder. Despite our best efforts not to be affected by the energies our pace had lifted, and we were walking faster.

We reached a small grove where the trees were thick and protective, and we sat down for a rest. Mrytle took this opportunity to tell us what she could about the energy we were experiencing. She was remembered the stories of a past time when a menacing energy had become so powerful by feeding on fear and hatred that it had almost decimated the human population. She recalled hearing how the creatures had somehow become trapped in this world that was not their home world. As the older generations of humans died out their beliefs in energetic being and the spiritual side of life died along with them. The Hunti, we did not know this is what they were called, had decreased in numbers and it was said that there were few of them left at all but in the years gone by the Hunti had been a powerful force of pure hate. They became weaker as the humans believed less in the esoteric side of life and therefore were less and less afraid of anything outside what they could hear and see.

We wondered who and what they were and why they were here, now, chasing us. What did they want with us? At this time, we had no idea it was the Chest that we had unearthed that they were looking for.

ARRIVAL IN JOANNAMERE

We knew we were near to the safety of the city of Joannamere, King Lombrox and his family were our clan. Bolstered by this knowledge we headed off singing loudly as we trotted along. Soon we saw the open mouths of the caves ahead of us and with one last chorus and nervous laughter we tumbled into the caves.

To our immense relief, we noticed that the energies did not follow us into the caves. We had no idea why, but we guessed they did not like the darkness, we were very thankful for this. Myrtle would record this weakness just as she would begin to correlate all info from the past to figure out what or who was behind this attack. The sweet earthy smells and the mustiness and the darkness of the caves wrapped around us like a security blanket, and we sat on the ground to have a rest after our running, this enforced rest also allowed the time needed for our eyes to become adjusted to the darkness and our bodies to the thick black air of the caves.

The river dwellers in Joannamere were of the Elan Clan so we were sure of our welcome, they would be pleased to see us, too pleased, in fact, we had no time to be distracted from our journey. We also understood the tradition of the giving and taking of hospitality. This was especially important in dwarfdom. We had to tread carefully to keep and if possible, improve the respect of the family ties but we also had to ensure our mission was not stalled a minute longer than necessary. We were determined to get on our way as quickly as we could. Our little party swelled as we got closer to the centre of the city, the word had spread. They had heard us coming. Our approach had not been discreet. Families gladly came out to meet us as excited children ran here and there, laughing and tumbling in their excitement. It was the greeting we needed and soon we were relaxed and confident again.

The women of Joannamere were happy to see their clanswomen and Myrtle, Frurose and Pria were being pulled in all directions. The men just hugged us, wrestled with us in a friendly manner and carried us all further into the city. Finally, we all reached the Grand Hall. What an impressive site the Hall was. It simply took your breath away, but we however were not able to get a good look at all of it due to the amount of our kin who jostled, slapped, pushed and half carried us along until we reached the end of the Great Hall, where King Lombrox was waiting for us.

King Lombrox greeted us heartily. It was hard not to stare in amazement or indeed to turn and run as he came rushing towards us. He was as tall as our King Paelion but not as broad. His arms in his sleeveless vest were muscular as was his whole body. His hands were huge. Red curly hair fell down his back but the top and sides were shaven. His long beard was caught just below his chin with a leather thong. His eyes were emerald, green. They were glinting with excitement as those arms and hands embraced us in a huge, welcoming hug. We were lucky to come out of the hug alive.

Aware of his curiosity as to our mission I opened my satchel as soon as I was able to do so and handed him the parchment scroll that King Paelion had given me for him. I do not know the contents of this letter, but after he had read it, he simply nodded at me, and he gestured for us to prepare for lunch. We were led by a small group of giggling women to a washstand where with their help we managed to remove a good deal of the journey's grime. Later we would bathe in the wonderful, underground hot springs.

The inhabitants of Joannamere had been following our movements and thus were expecting us, a delicious looking, and smelling, feast was laid out on the longest table I had ever seen. The table was fashioned from a tree trunk which had fallen into the cavern, it was lying on its' side, and the top had been sliced off to create the massive table. Moss grew along the sides and small flowering plants clung to the bark. It was exceptionally beautiful. The table was laden with delicacies that were favoured among dwarves, a spread we were eager to sample after our days of walking and eating from our packs. One of our most loved foods was in good supply.

Fungi, of all types, both common and prized sprung up here and there in the crevasses of the bark on the table side, and others had been gathered from near and far. Meats from small animals that live underground, animals like snakes and grubs and delicious looking lizards. Larger prey from the surface was also included. Trays of venison and wild boar amongst the delicious spread before us. There were grasses and fruits, and a wide variety of flowers all presented in a beautiful smorgasbord.

It is well known that dwarves like to live under earth, that we are not surface dwellers but while we do not seek light, we do not shun it either and indeed use it to our advantage. We do have farmers that farm on the surface of the land. Underearth, we make light shafts in the rock face to bring rays of sun into the depths. With this light we can grow food, usually a series of grasses and vegetables. The darkness also produces its bounty. Unusual species of fungi grow underground. Mosses and grasses feed on the fungi as well. Roots of surface plants penetrating down into the caves created the perfect environment for these to blossom.

Dwarfs are a clean and hygienic, contrary to stories otherwise, and we use very inventive methods to keep our underground cities clean. Waste shafts supply all waste into a huge furnace metre below, these wastes fuel the fires for cooking and heating, and they also fuel the forges for the blacksmiths to make the metal armour and weapons that the dwarfs use in battle. Other innovative products such as pots, pans, utensils, and decorative ornaments were fashioned in the forges.

THE LEGEND OF THE LOMBROX BRIDGE

We left the hospitality of our kinsmen and reached the Lombrox Bridge. As we crossed the bridge, I recalled the most famous of King Lombrok's deeds. Over one hundred years ago raiders from across the North Sea decided to attack the humans and dwarf clans in search of new land gold and treasure. The Malchureans, their species was an unknown one to the humans and dwarfs that they attacked. They appeared to be neither human nor dwarf. They were taller than the humans and were hirsute, they were muscular but seemed to be slightly unbalanced in their gait. Their lower bodies being shorter than their torsos. This is all I know of them as this is what is recorded in the histories. After conquering all the villages that stood in their path, they arrived at Joannamere in an overconfident and jubilant manner. They entered the caves expectantly, but their forward momentum was abruptly halted when they were met by Lombrox and his warriors on the bridge. Lombrox left all except twenty of his men on the city side of the bridge while he and twenty of his fiercest warriors crossed to meet the army of thousands head on. The fighting was fierce, and hundreds of the attacking soldiers were now on the bridge along with the twenty, in the midst of all this Lombrox would call out, 'Now!' One man would flee across the bridge back into the cave system, and as he went, he slashed one of the ropes holding the bridge. The invading army would press them back and he would call for the next to go. Eventually they were close to their own side and the last of his soldiers ran back and slashed the second last rope. The bridge now hung by a thread. Lombrox took one more swing with his axe and took an almighty leap as the bridge gave way beneath their feet. His men managed to grab his arms as he grasped the rocky cliffs below the bridge. They pulled him up and the Malchurean army plummeted to their deaths. Those that did not perish retreated directly into King Paelion's army as he rode at haste to help Lombrox. This group never returned to try again, and the legend of Lombrox Bridge was recorded in history.

We reached this famous bridge as we journeyed out of Joannamere, eager to get back on our quest we were moving along at a good pace. There was a grassy bank to one side of the bridge so here I called a halt. I said, 'We will take a rest and a moment to reflect on the heroic deeds of our Clansman Lombrox' It is our duty to pay our respects and to think on this as we make our own choices along life's pathways.' We all took a seat on the grass and removed our headwear. Bowing our heads I prayed aloud for the same strength that Lombrox displayed when he saved the city and his Clan. After this brief time of reflection, we resumed our journey and began to cross the famous bridge. On my way across I imagined Lombrox and the battle that had taken place right here. I hoped if ever I was called upon, I could show such courage. Once across we picked up our pace and began to travel as quickly as we could along the underground pathways. We were happy and bolstered by the visit to our kinsmen and we laughed and joked as we walked. Here and there we ran into fungi gardens and their caretakers. After another three days of fast travel, we came upon a series of staircases hewn in the rock, they ran upward at an acute angle. Our pace was slowed by the steep climb but after a day's travel we could once more see the sunlight ahead of us and we stepped out to the sun and open land. Along the stairways leading to the surface, we encountered the constructed light shafts beaming into caves on each landing, in each was a garden basking in the sun light.

We had never questioned how the light penetrated so far into the underworld but as we were on a quest, nothing was taken for granted and we stopped to enquire from a lovely family of gardeners. Reflective light was the key and the placing of light reflectors, made from beaten gold sheets, placed at the correct angles allowed them to penetrate the darkness. In other places the light was reflected by huge crystals that had been mined in the underground quarries. The quality of light depended on the depth of the gardens, and this resulted in different plants on various levels. On this level not far below the surface delicious melons grew, and we feasted on these while we waited for our eyes to become adjusted to the outside light, we also began to discuss our path onward.

We had generously been given supplies to bring on our journey, among these were rare fungi – this particular fungus was highly nutritious, full of energy and incredibly good for hard, fast travel. These fungi, however, could have a potentially disastrous effect. It is harvested when the light of the outer sun is at its peak and the energy of this sun joins with the earth energies to form a powerful truth telling essence. The fungus can only be eaten with a pure heart and if not, it is fatal. It is a credit to my team that we all tucked in heartily every night.

We were still a long way from the human city of Cam, but we were travelling along at a good pace. Our conversation involved discussions around our being able to enter the city when we arrived. Even when we reached the walls of the city, we had not yet managed to devise a way in. Ten dwarfs marching to the gate seemed to be a little risky. We must produce a plan. After giving this a great amount of our time and energies we had no answer so we decided to get as close as we could to the city and see if a way to get inside presented itself to us.

UNDER ATTACK AGAIN

We were in this relaxed and comfortable frame of mind as we walked along the edge of a great wood. We kept to the edge for cover and shade, but it was easier to walk where the trees and fallen branches were not so thick. Suddenly Elkfast's shrill hiss and raised hand had us all frozen in our tracks. Whispering to us he said that he had sensed something or things approaching us from within the forest. He estimated they, or it, were a good distance from us, however whatever it was it had our scent and was in search of us. He asked the trees to help us by hindering the path of our pursuers and clearing our way forward. We could not decide whether concealment was our best options, or to run as fast and seek an underground passage or cave. Hiding would not conceal our scent and climbing the trees was not really an option, we were small in stature, and climbing was not something we were great at, and we had no idea if going up a tree would provide a way of escape. We had little time to decide what to do so we ran!

We ran as fast as we could and it was a good pace, Pria because of her size was falling behind so I slowed down to let her catchup with me, I planned to stay with her and I urged the others to continue as fast as they could, however Dwaymoon was not having that, and he scooped Pria up over his shoulder and simply took her with him, he was strong and she was tiny, I did not protest but increased my own pace to keep us all together. Myrtle, our keeper of histories, was scanning her memories for any records we had of our pursuers, as we ran. She was also searching for a tunnel or a cave we could slip far enough into to evade our enemy. As I ran, I wished I knew what I was running from. We were not afraid of a fight and if it became necessary that is what we would do. Our main intent was to reach Cam and the dragons so we wished to avoid anything that would threaten that outcome. But if it came down to a fight well, we would be up for a good one.

Looking back at the forests edge I glimpsed our pursuers. Immediately I saw them wished I did not know what was chasing us. These predators where not something I had seen and although Myrtle searched her histories and had found little information, the information she did find she was not able to share as she did not have time. She was concentrating on finding us an escape route. We could hear what she had learned later if there was a later for us.

A pack of large dogs, I counted at least fifteen, were running at us. The dogs, apart from shouldering overly big heads, were long and lean and they were deep golden in colour. Their chests were large, and their bodies thinned out at the back. Standing about one metre at the shoulder they were as tall as we were. Long muscular leg powered their pursuit, and they looked fit and healthy. They seemed to understand how to hunt as they had spread out to come around us and were gaining ground with every step. Should I make the call, stand and fight now, while I could use the bowmen to useful effect, or keep trying to escape? All these questions were flashing through my mind. Just as I had made the decision that we would have to make a stand and start shooting, Myrtle yelled for us to turn sharply to our left, in a hundred steps there was a small tunnel leading to an underwater aquifer. We could fit in but single file, and we would then only have to defend the entrance. I instructed with a yell for the smaller team members to go in and go back as far as they could. Elzer was to go in behind them, Hegal and me following close behind.

As we were running at full speed Elzar was setting his bow to fight as soon as we hit the tunnel.

Dwaymoon pushed Pria unceremoniously down the tunnel and then stood at the door with Elzar, ready to fight if necessary. He and Elzar dove in as soon as the rest of the party was out of sight and Hegal and I straight behind them. Elzar's first arrow found its mark on the leading dog, not eight feet behind us. The other bowmen now were able to step up and send their arrows as well. Although our arrows were accurate and were meeting their mark, the dogs were not slowing down and by now were at the opening to the tunnel. Thankfully, the mouth was only about one step wide and was defendable by two of us, standing shoulder to shoulder. Elzar and Treeturn continued to shoot in the limited space he found to get passed Hegal. This made the difference as Hegal, and I chopped and hacked at dog after dog. While I was standing so close to the dogs, I noticed they had a smaller eye in the centre of their foreheads, and they did not have ears only an elongated hole where an ear could be expected to be.

They did not give up when wounded instead seemed to be even more intent on killing us. Every few minutes Hegal and I changed places with the other warriors to keep our strength up and increase our defence as well as we could. Eventually their numbers began to dwindle and when only about six remained standing they appeared to have been disturbed by something else and they halted their attack on us. After studying what they had seen or heard they began to run off. They pushed and pulled at their fallen as if trying to check if they were dead, then they moved back toward the forest, stopping often to look back toward us and whatever else had intervened on our behalf. We had not seen them, but a small group of Metungians were walking by, and their sheer size had been enough for the dogs to seek cover.

Even though we were very curious as to why the dogs had suddenly run off, we decided to stay in the tunnel for a while. The tunnel went back a long way, and Myrtle was able to tell us that it was a formed by water running out of the underground river when it overflowed its banks. The water was low at this time, so we were safe form this danger. Leaving the entrance guarded the rest of us walked back to check our injuries, find the water and to cleanse ourselves after the fighting. I had three or four deep gashes on my arms but most of the blood on me was not my own. The attackers had not got off lightly and been severely injured. Hegal and the others were the same, we all had cuts and bites. Frurose and Dwaymoon went to work cleansing our wounds, even though they too were cut and bitten. They used all their healing powers and herbal remedies to fight off any infection and to speed our healing. After we had a good long time of washing in the water. I made the decision to stay underground and sleep, we could not stay too long as we did not want to be still there if the dogs returned in numbers, but right now we needed to rest.

Myrtle was looking for other options for us to use to escape if they came back when we left the safety of the tunnel. We could not stay here for long. We hoped by sneaking away in the dark of night and by using herbs and other concealment methods we could cover our tracks. We could use potions made by Frurose to cover our scent as well. We took turns to keep a watch and to sleep, hours later, and as soon as the light of the outer sun had gone down, we crept out of the tunnel.

Although we travelled with our senses on high alert and kept a good ear out for anything unusual, we heard nothing that night and by morning a return to normal had settled over our walking. As we walked Myrtle told us about the animals that had attacked us. These were racing dogs that had been left behind when the Portal closed years ago. They had not been hunting dogs and had not had to fend for themselves at all. Once abandoned either by choice or consequence they had survived as they could, scavenging and learning to hunt. They had to fight other predators along the way, they had returned to the most basic instinct of survival.

AN ENCOUNTER
WITH GIANTS

After a couple of undisturbed hours of walking, we saw a group of giants sleeping near the edge of a rocky outcrop. We stopped abruptly and froze instinctively. We did not know they were the ones who had startled the dogs and scared them off, but we thought it most likely. We realised we could not stay frozen forever so we began to walk on as quietly as we could. Unfortunately, the giants had a guard watching over their campsite and he rose up off the ground in front of us. Myrtle had worked out that they were Metungians, and she said this aloud to us as he approached us. He smiled and bent down and extended his huge hand towards us. Not sure what to do, as I only came up to his knee, I jumped onto his hand, and he lifted me up to his eye level. This amused him and a great bellow of laughter came out of his wide mouth. I would fit in that mouth I thought.

Myrtle, who had been rapidly scanning for information on these amazing people, reassured me that I was not going to be eaten. She addressed the giant in a language I did not understand but he did. He bent down and with his other hand lifted her up as well, so that he could hear her clearly. Impressed by her ability to speak his native language he replied, they then established that the rest of us could not understand, so they began to converse in our language, which to my surprise he understood and spoke very clearly. He asked us about the encounter with the dogs, and we told him that happened. By now all the giants were waking up and soon we were surrounded. More of the giants bent down and picked one or more of us up. It was funny and undignified at the same time, but I realised by the conversation that they were doing this so they could hear us. The knew we were dwarves and had a fair bit of understanding of who we were and what we did. They invited us to share their breakfast, and we agreed, we were still a bit shaken, and a rest would do us good. Our wounds were checked and pronounced to be treated as well as could be out here. We shared with them briefly what we were doing up above the ground and they wished us luck on our quest. They began a long discussion amongst themselves to which we listened intently but discreetly, we did not want to be caught eaves dropping, we did not understand what the topic of their conversation was. They then told us that there was a member of their family living in Cam, he was called Tanir, we would know him if we saw him. He was working in Cam managing their exceptionally large War Beasts.

After enjoying a huge breakfast of all sorts of fruit and different breads and cheeses with the giants, they prepared to leave us head north and to their home in the mountains, they told us what they knew about the dogs, having encountered them many times as they explored the planet. The thought it was unusual that we had been attacked as they did not usually attack people but as were smaller than most other species it is possible they thought we were game, and our scent would have been unfamiliar to them as well. There was only this one pack in existence on Pardow as far as they knew, and we would be out of their territory by now. They were sure we would be safe from further attacks from the dogs. We were about to depart from their company when two of the giant Metungians decided to walk along with us, they asked if we were agreeable to the two of them walking with us to Cam. They had decided to travel to Cam and if it were possible without causing too much alarm amongst the citizens of Cam, they would visit Tanir.

We walked along with them until they, unfortunately, had to admit that our small steps made it difficult for them. After some laughter and discussion as to finding a way to carry us all, they decided to walk ahead and promised that they would return if they encountered anything they perceived dangerous to us. Being carried would have been expedient but not dignified. We were warriors after all. We said our goodbyes and expressed a hope that we would see them in Cam. Two such allies may be of use.

With this exciting start to the day lifting our spirits we left the company of the last two giants. We had lost time, but we had gained information and made useful friends. We continued to be observant despite our buoyant mood and eventually the conversation returned once again to our main problem, that of getting into the city of Cam. As the day progressed, we began to see more humans out, and about their business. We decided to once more move into the shadowy edge of the forest. As we walked along our small stature and dark, natural, clothing fitted in with the dappled light of the forests, even in quite low growth we had good cover, and we could see any humans from a great distance. They were tall, noisy, and easy to hear and see, when we did, we simple melted back into the undergrowth. The humans passed within feet of us, they did not appear to have any sense of their surroundings, and their minds and conversations were taken up by thoughts of home and supper and wives or husbands and focused on possessions and pleasures, whatever provided them some form of comfort, distraction and entertainment.

In around seven days with this cautious but uninterrupted pace we reached the outskirts of Cam. We had not been attacked again by the dogs, and we had not experienced the strange energetic beings that had menaced us before we got to Joannamere, and the home of the King Lombrok. Now as we got closer to Cam, we sensed the energetic beings again. A strange feeling of disquiet came over us, we all sensed it. Elzar had had a feeling of immense hatred in the forest of Ainslia and now it was back and was even more intense as we moved forward. We did not know anything concrete about our enemy, but we knew for sure someone, or something, was just as interested in our quest as we were. They, it, whatever it was, it was following us.

GETTING INTO
THE CITY OF CAM

The outskirts of the city spread before us as far as we could see. We could see the massive gates ahead of us. There was a collection of ramshackle houses and huts, gardens and workhouses in between us and the entrance to Cam. Dogs, goats, chickens, and children ran hither and thither, they were all scruffy and unkempt. Here and there the youngsters were working but most were happily enjoying their day. Men and women walked here and there, going about their daily business. All seemed peaceful and unthreatening in this part of the city, but it did not appear the same inside the gates. For here inside, dominating everything else around, was the massive inner-city walls. These walls seemed to reach to the sky, they were constructed with huge rocks, which had been chiselled into squares. The walls appeared impenetrable, and we immediately knew we would not get into the inner city without outside help or a risky enterprise of our own devices. We had come so far, we did not know what depended on us finding the secret to the Chest, but we did know that the King himself had sent us, we must not fail. There had to be a way.

We set up a rough camp at the edge of the forest and blended in with the undergrowth. Here we remained unnoticed. We set a watch, while the remainder of our party settled down for a well-deserved rest. My mind was racing so I volunteered to be part of the first watch. I would not have been able to sleep anyway. Hegel and Treeturn stayed up with me, and we discussed, thought of, and discarded over and over ways to get into the city. We changed watch throughout the day and eventually I fell into a light sleep. At nightfall we waited until the darkness was complete and made our way up to the outer wall. It was as solid as it looked.

We returned to our cover in the early hours of the morning and sat down to plan. We looked at what we had and looked at the wall. Even when we worked out a way in, we would be faced with unknown obstacles on the inside.

We would have to take any opportunities that presented themselves to us. We talked of ways to use the individual talents of the team. We also decided to try to at least make positive efforts to get in. One talent we all had in common was to mine, to dig. We decided our best option was to do what dwarfs do best. We would tunnel in, tunnelling in would also give us a way out. A tunnel under the wall and the city seemed out best plan. The next night we walked the perimeter of the wall again and diligently searched. Our efforts were rewarded, and we found the best place to begin. A waterway with solid iron gates we thought may provide us a viable way through the outer walls and we would then have an opportunity to see where we needed to go from there. If we needed to tunnel, we did not know for how long and for how far or what direction.

The city was impressive. The walls that surrounded the outer city were made up of huge blocks of stone as high and as long as a carriage.

They were stacked twenty high and appeared to go up and up forever. Crowds came and went. In and out of the city gates they spilled, people of all different shapes and sizes. Many of the inhabitants were dressed in attire we had never witnessed, and we assumed they had come in from the regions around Cam. There were groups that were clearly not human.

I made the decision to split our group up, most of the team began working on the waterway and because we needed more information about the city, inside the walls, so we also decided that five of us, Myrtle, Elzar, Myself and Pria and Treeturn would simply walk in. Dwaymoon was keen to join us, and I knew his concerns were for Pria's safety. I reassured him as best I could, but I had chosen my best team for this part of the journey, and I could not make changes for the sake of personal feelings.

Reluctantly Dwaymoon joined those working on the waterway gates which were quickly breached and the men soon found it was, as we had suspected, connected to a large cave system. This was great news and was it relayed to me via Elzar who we had taken with us so that he could go between us to report what was happening in each group. Hegal returned to our main group to inform them of our plan to attempt to gain entry to the outer city simply by walking through the gates. There was a small hope that we could meld with others coming in and out and go unnoticed amongst Cam's diverse population. Whatever we chose to do was fraught with obstacles, but we had to try something. This was not a time for hesitancy, and it is not in a dwarf's nature to give in or up.

I, Myrtle, Elzar, Pria and Treeturn sat motionless all day and listened and observed the people the coming and goings, but the gates remained closed. They did not open all day.

We had just decided to return to the edge of a forest that night, thinking that the idea to walk in was not going to be successful, when the large gates in front of our vantage point opened and a column of men marched out. They had large dogs with them. Dogs we knew and understood. Elzar had sensed then immediately, and they had sensed him and now of course us as well. We hurriedly devised a new plan. Treeturn would make a covering spell to hide Elzar and Myrtle by turning them into dogs, this would hide them from the men, the dogs would be harder to fool. Treeturn and Priya and I would remain outside the spell. As we got closer to the gates Treeturn used her changeling strengths to take on the form of a dog herself so she could simply walk alongside us, and we would walk into the city. We hoped the dogs would accept her and not make a fuss about her or Elzar and Myrtle hiding behind Treeturn's masking spell.

The five of us, me Pria and a large, attractive hound, stepped out of the bush and onto the path. Myrtle and Elzar under the masking spell came along a short distance behind us. The astonished looks on the faces of the soldiers turned to confusion at the sight of Pria and Me. It is reasonable to consider that the majority were unlikely to have ever seen a Dwarf. Not having any way to tell just what we were they became aggressive and decided to accompany us along the way. They quickly surrounded us. An old man of unusual description, and a child with her dog should have been innocent enough but they were taking no chances with us. We offered no resistance as this was what we needed to happen. It was a way through the gates. From their conversation we understood that the soldiers intended to take us to the King's guard for his assessment. We were marched into the city and Treeturn mingled with the dogs and came in with us. Elzar and Myrtle moved away from us after entering the city and they mingled with the crowds. Myrtle was already mentally mapping the city adding any knew information to that which we already had. As were being moved along we noticed a group of Elves staring at us with undisguised suspicion, they knew we were Dwarves, but they held their peace and their tongues.

Thornfoot paused in his retelling of the story, he needed a drink and a small rest. The servants rushed off to bring all of them more refreshments and Thornfoot closed his eyes and relaxed. During this break, the dragons and servants talked and laughed and recounted to each other what they thought of the journey so far. The dragons got to their feet and stretched their wings. After having a drink of delicious mead and being offered a tray of cakes, which he ate heartily, Thornfoot continued the story.

CAM

The city was large and spread out and distinct groups had found a niche for themselves within its walls. We knew from our research of Cam that a large community of Elves lived in a remote part of the city, beyond the upper walls of the inner city. The community was led by five 'Elders' and these positions were usually passed down from generation to generation. The Elders were indeed quite old. Caro was one of two elders who were young in comparison to the others, she along with her partner Eisvold had recently had the roles passed down to them.

The area in which the Elves lived was a mountainous region that was separated by a series of large lakes from the rest the city's inhabitants. The Elves roamed freely and ruled themselves. An agreement with former kings had made this possible. They agreed that they would use their military prowess on the side of Cam if it ever found itself at war with another city. This had never happened because of the dragons in the city's artillery. Thus, they lived a secure lifestyle. They did as they chose here in their allocated lands and were a strong and useful community. Elves are renowned for their skills as archers and for their speed on foot, a handy talent in battle.

They were an accepted part of the city's different ethnic groups. The elves grew fruits and vegetables and sold these to the city dwellers. They also made and sold beautiful ornaments and drawings. The younger Elves, in an attempt at more connection to the human population had established a business producing Elvin cosmetics and medications. Essences taken from the plants and trees. The skin products were immensely popular with the human women as they wished to have the soft youthful skin of an elf. Caro was one elf that believed in harmony with the human population, she believed that their own survival in Cam depended on this relationship. Caro liked to help with the elderly in the elven community and with the humans and other groups in Cam. Everyone enjoyed her visits and called out greetings to her as she came down the roads. She would deliver fresh fruit and vegetables to those unable to produce their own. She helped with the injured and sick. Using her herbal remedies and her natural healing skills. Caro was a fiercely proud elf, she was a strong warrior, preferring the bow as her weapon but she was not slow on her feet and would take the battlefield if necessary. She had fought in the last Dwarf versus Elf war. Her personal beliefs were that war was not the way to solve problems and believed love and honest communication was better than fighting. If her family were threatened however, she would fight, without hesitation, for them.

Elves have an extremely long-life span, ten times longer than the average human, then, it is believed, that they simply move behind the veil that separates this life from the next and go on living indefinitely. The elves could choose for themselves only once when they wanted to be born into the physical and once to return to the life before this. The longevity gave them great insights as to the world and they knew and understood the histories of the groups around them. They remembered the Portal and its uses. They kept much of this to themselves. On occasions they would advise the King as to historic events and legends from the past.

THORNFOOT
CONTINUES
HIS STORY

After they had all had a time of rest and refreshment Thornfoot went on.

'As we came through the gate, we noticed the outer city was not as ramshackle as other human cities we had experienced. The gates were wide, and the guards appeared to uninterested in who came in and out. This was a city that was not expecting any attack or intruder, big or small. The city was orderly and neat. The roadways and paths were wide and appeared to be in orderly rows circling around the inner city The usual stench of human waste was not instantly apparent. Filth was not being poured into the roadways as we had been warned. The houses had thatched roofs and were picturesque in appearance

The inner city was different, here the gate guards were very efficient, checking everyone as they went passed. Luckily, we did not need to enter through these gates. We could see miles and miles of red roofs spiralling up the hill. At the centre and at the top of the hill King Elgrade's castle towered above us, standing proudly overlooking the city and the countryside for miles around.'

'Although humans were the predominate species in Cam in this period of history, they were not the only inhabitants. I noticed one group of very unusual beings standing, talking together, they were also dotted here and there throughout the wider community. They were about 5 ft tall and looked very reptilian. I suppose I was staring as one of them gave me a wave and pointed at me as if to say, 'I don't know what you are either.' They had smaller upper bodies and larger lower bodies; it was hard to tell exactly what was larger because they wore robes that covered them to their feet. The usual garb worn by the majority of the inhabitants of Cam was shirts, or vest and breaches or riding trousers for the men and depending on what the women were doing at the time they were much the same, occasionally there was a flowing skirt on a lady. I asked Myrtle as to what or who they were and she said she could not talk to me know as she was, if I had forgotten, a dog right now, she need her energy to uphold the illusion and she was also working on the city mapping'.

'Once inside we were inside the outer city walls Pria began to talk to the leader, her voice was as soft as a gentle summer breeze and full of persuasion, he could not resist. She told him I was the one they needed to punish. With her soft voice and tears flowing freely she told him she was being held captive by me. He became engrossed in her plight as she described me as the villain and that it would be fitting and fun to throw me into the dragons' lair. Why waste time on me? I was a troublemaker. Convinced that there was no need to take me to the Kings' guard, the leader shouted at the men that were holding me and told them to take me directly to the Diamond Cavern and get rid of me. It gave them all a good laugh to think of my predicament when I came face to face with the dragons. They decided to put me on the food elevator and send me down to be eaten. Of course, all of them were under the influence of Pria's voice and later when they realised what they had done they would be so horrified that they would never mention it again. Not even to each other.

Treeturn had come to lay at Pria's feet, and the leader of the men just smiled at them and told her to go home as if she were an errant child, which she had persuaded him she was. She trotted off with the dog following. I stole a quick glance backwards towards Elzar's hiding spot and saw him trot off, back toward the rest of the team. When I looked back at Elzar I noticed a bird like man, well I'm not sure but I saw a tallish man who appeared to have a feathered head and a beak instead of a nose, he was looking at me with keen interest, so I quickly turned away. I made a mental note to remember that this was another thing I needed an explanation from Myrtle but now was not the time.

I was being pushed, shoved, and forced along at a pace my short legs could hardly keep up with, but I did not mind at all as I was heading for Diamond Cavern and the legendary dragons of Cam. I could not have been happier. Pria and Treeturn, who had returned to his usual form, followed at a safe distance mapping directions to the hidden chamber where I was taken. Tomorrow when the gates were opened, they would leave the city and rejoin our party. Who would take any notice of a child and her dog going out to the fields to collect mushrooms?

I had made it into the Dragon Cavern, and I was so excited to ascertain that there really were dragons under the city of Cam. The legends were real. I was filled with relief and intrepidation, but excitement was what I felt most, and this overrode all my fears.'

When Thornfoot reached the end of this detailed account of the amazing journey they had all undertaken and how they had managed to get him inside the Cavern, the dragons all began to laugh uproariously. Shari exclaimed, 'What a clever plot. But I am not sure if it was really a good plot for how are you to get out? No one gets out of this cavern. Even our slaves are locked in with us. There is no way out and believe me if there was, we would know about it.' The dragons looked worried, and saying nothing about this concern to Thornfoot they suggested that he take a well-earned rest while they took time to contemplate his long story. They would also contemplate the consequences of the Chest being discovered.

THE DRAGON'S
DECIDE

Thornfoot slept on a rocky ledge, far above the ground, where he would not get stepped on by a pacing dragon. It was obvious to him that the dragons were agitated and what he had told them had caused them to be genuinely concerned. He decided to give them their own time and truthfully, he had no choice, he had no way to manipulate a dragon. He felt his own character was on the line here. He had spoken the truth, and he hoped he could rely on their natural ability to see the heart and that they would judge his pure and worthy. The Dwarf Clan was desperately in need of the dragons help and advice.

He slept and he dreamed. He dreamt he was at home with his wife, he dreamt that his bed was soft and warm, and that he held his sweetheart close to him. His heart was full, they had been together throughout their lives and had grown older together. He longed for the comfortable comradery they had shared. They no longer needed words to communicate, and he heard and felt her voice often during the journey. And although he was honoured and happy and excited by the amazing quest he was on. He missed her. He hoped to be in her arms, in their home, soon. He hoped to be alive to achieve this and in one piece, for a start.

There was a stirring below and he woke with a start from his ponderings. He felt himself being shaken, at first, he thought there was an earth tremor in one of the mining shafts and was immediately on full alert but then he became aware of where he was and realised the dragons were approaching his resting place on the ledge. He came back to the reality of the Cavern and his mission.

Josepheos led the dragons, and he told Thornfoot their decision was in his favour, 'We have decided! We will help you! But we must find a way to escape our prison, we must find a pathway out of the Cavern. We know what is in the Chest, but we will not tell you or anyone else, until we are safely out of here. There are other reasons, but the most determining one right know is that walls have ears. We must guard this information at all costs for it could mean our lives and indeed yours as well. We will go with you back to King Paelion but first we must find the Great Sea Dragon Thesso. He will decide what we will do with the Chest. This is his creation, and he will know what to do. '

He looked directly into Thornfoot's eyes and asked, 'So how do we get out of this place?'

ESCAPE FROM DIAMOND CAVERN AND THE CITY OF CAM

Thornfoot was so excited he danced excitedly around on the ledge. He did not know who Thesso was, but he knew that the dragons here trusted him, and if finding him solved the question of opening the Chest then he was happy to accommodate this in his plans. He did not dwell of any of this now as he was eager to part with his incredibly good news. He almost shouted when he said, 'I am sure you know that dwarves love to tunnel, and digging is a skill we have, and we love. Ever since I entered the city with Pria the rest of my party have been tunnelling toward us here in this cavern. They have been joined with every available dwarf from the Lombrok clan as well, and all have been desperately digging and tunnelling toward us. If you listen, you can hear the rhythm of the shovels and picks.'

Thornfoot explained further, 'They have met resistance in a formation of a wide rocky wall along the riverbank at the beginning of the work. To not make it obvious that the wall is being breached they have dug under the rock so that they can crawl further inside the cavern before they started their digging in earnest. Once they were under this rock wall, they were able to follow the wider caverns of the river path and then finally there is one smaller wall of stone to conquer, and they will be here. It should not be too long now. Frurose has been keeping in mind contact with me as to their progress. Pria is also walking in and out of the city gates with Treeturn alongside. They have been carrying information back and forth to Frurose as well.' Treeturn was disguising himself as a faithful pet but every now and again he would forget what dog he was the day before and this caused confused looks from the guards as they strolled through the gates.

Thornfoot continued, 'As you can see from all of this it will not be long and we will have a way of escape, so we need to be ready to go. I am hoping that you will still be able to fly.'

The dragons responded by yelling in unison. 'Yes, we can fly as we have the amazing exercise machine designed and built especially for us by King Elgrade.' The King had thought to increase the wind speed in one of the underground chambers by creating a wind tunnel. A series of huge fans at one end of the chamber has been installed. 'These fans combined to provide a powerful wind force which allows us to fly in place. The fans are connected to a series of cogs and wheels back to the surface where another set of fans spins continuously in the breeze. These surface fans are set on a high hill which had been formed for the purpose. It is an ingenious system and works perfectly. There is no room for dipping and diving, but it does give us space to keep our wings strong. He wants us to always to be battle ready and thus keeps us fit, we are also well fed, therefore we are both physically strong and healthy.'

Thornfoot was pleased by this revelation, but he had another concern. He lowered his voice to a hushed whisper. 'What about the servants? I have no wish to do harm to anyone, but it would be wise to silence them permanently or take them with us. It will make our escape so much more difficult if we take prisoners. There is really no choice in this as none can remain behind. News of our escape will be best kept secret as long as possible and we do not need anyone knowing of my being here, and thus the Dwarf Clan's part in your escape. Nor do we want anyone else knowing about the Chest until we know what it is we are dealing with.'

The dragons agreed with this but felt comfortable that the servants, who had lived in the caves with the dragons for years, would come with them willingly. There was no need for giving them the ultimation of death if they did not come. It was decided that Thornfoot would hold an audience with the servants one at a time, or in family groups. He would ask them the question and then once they agreed to the journey out of the caverns, they would stay in this one chamber until the rescuers broke through the final rock wall and departure was imminent. If they did not agree they would be taken to a different chamber. Thornfoot was very relieved and thankful when they all agreed to the escape and the journey to freedom with the dragons. They loved the dragons as they had cared for them for years. They also wanted their own freedom.

After two more days impatiently waiting, they heard the picks, everyone moved quickly back toward the farther edge of the cavern away from the walls as they began to crack. Suddenly a dusty dwarf head popped through the wall, a huge grin on his dirty face, then increasingly as the rocks gave way to the picks and shovels.

All these dusty heads stopped and stared in awe at the three dragons. Then Elzar broke the spell as he shouted out to the watching dragons, 'Are you coming with us?'

'Yes! Yes! Yes,' the dragons yelled back in unison.'

Elzar turned his head back to the wall, he shouted to the workers. 'We're going to need a bigger hole.' With laughter and renewed enthusiasm, they began the task of expanding the height and width of the escape route.

It would take two or three days to ensure the escape route through the caverns was large enough for the huge dragons to comfortable get through to the outer wall. The very last section of the rock face would remain untouched until they were all assembled and ready to leave the cave. There was a significant party to evacuate the cave. The Dwarves began to work again and the teams that were resting tried to do just that.

Ledges were cleared and soft clothes were laid out for the tired bodies. They would sleep and work in shifts. The air was tense with excitement and adrenaline. There was also fear and dread as all were aware that exposure would be fatal. All of this coupled with anticipation and hope made sleeping difficult.

During this waiting time I sat with the dragons and with Hegal as we tried to plan out our movements once leaving the caves. Other dwarfs who had come to help with the digging and members of our original team sat in on the discussions, adding what they thought may be of importance or helpful. We examined the maps and drawings we had brought along with us on the journey and the dragons recalled and remembered what they had seen in the past. Myrtle wrote down all the information that they were able to add and drew maps up with the dragons' guidance. Finally, a direction was decided on, and a plan formed.

Josepheos, the oldest of the dragons said, 'We must immediately send a team back to Christiana to inform King Elon to be prepared for our arrival. We will also need to make him aware of the need for us to take the Chest from his custody and return it to Thesso the great

Sea Dragon. We will explain everything when we arrive in Christiana. We must ensure that King Paelion understands the importance of us taking the Chest to Thesso. The Clan Elan must be ready to assist our quick passage, and they must also prepare for a battle which will surely follow our escape. It is of extreme urgency that the Chest is immediately surrendered to us. Those following you and soon us as well, will follow where the Chest goes so, they at least are not going to attack Christiana but there are other forces and beings that will want access to the Chest and will seek knowledge at whatever cost. King Elgrade himself will be seeking revenge, and he will not allow our escape without pursuit.'

'Thornfoot, your team knows the route so Hegel and one other should head off as soon as possible. They should not stop at Lombrok. Speed is our priority; we must make haste to get our message through. It would be perfect if they are safely in Christiana by the time King Elgrade finds out we are gone.' At this point Thornfoot was happy to have something to add.

'We have been working on an escape plan if one became necessary and Pria has been working on different ideas within the walls of Cam. One of these ideas is an exit plan that we could put into action very quickly should it be needed, and I think it will be perfect to get Hegal, and I will send Elkfast with him, out of the city and off to Christiana with haste. I will send word to her now and she will meet Hegal and Elkfast in the forest across from the rock face later today.'

Inside the walls of the city of Cam Pria and Treeturn had once more found the Metungians and had been socialising with them as they strolled around enjoying the unusual sights of the outer city. Pria had also been spending time each day at the King's stables, playing with her pet dog, who of course was Treeturn in disguise. She talked to the guards and shared her lunch with them. She always used her most persuasive voice when talking to the guards, and they were now comfortable and happy in her company. Often, they bought small toys for her to play with. Treeturn was always in the shape of a dog when others were around, and the guards liked to give him a treat and pat him. He had finally gotten used to which dog he had formed in which place he was. Here, at the stables, he was a large wolfhound, one of his favourite shapes. After lunch Pria and Treeturn always left the stables and would go for a walk out of the city to meet up with Elkfast and exchange what was learnt or needed sometimes the Metungians accompanied them. Their size gave them reassurance that they would not be challenged.

Today, like always the guards played a game of dice, they laughed and drank and often dozed off. Late in the day when the game was well under away and a handful of guards were snoring loudly, she and Treeturn, who now was in the shape of one of the stable hands, returned to the stables. It was just before the closing of the city gates for the night. The guards that were still sober and playing dice and took no notice of them. They quickly saddled up two of the horses These they had picked out over the last weeks as they knew them to and steady beasts. But also, able to move quickly. Pria had persuaded the stable hands to house them at the end of the stable and nearest to the doors, out of the sight of the back room where the men usually played and drank. The guards and stable hands got more drunk and played their game very loudly. Pria and the disguised Treeturn crept passed them toward the door only to find it locked. This was unusual because she had checked their routine every night, however, for whatever reason they had locked up early tonight. Fortunately for her she was able to slip through the railings and ran quickly to seek out the Metungians for help. Due to their size, they created interest wherever they were, so she sought out the biggest crowds and soon spotted them standing head and shoulder above the others in the crowd. Signalling to them to come she asked them to return to the stables with her which they happily obliged and they were able to quickly snap the locks on the gates, so Pria and the stableboy were able to bring the horses through. The Metungians did not ask questions as to what they were doing as they knew the dwarfs were unlikely to tell them anyway. Pria and Treeturn stealthily lead the horses away. The Metungians walked them to the gate and then mingled back with the residents of the city. At the gates Pria and Treeturn simply walked through. It was late, no one wanted to challenge anyone. The men just wanted to go home for their supper. Once out of sight of the walls she and Treeturn hopped onto the horses and sped off to the meeting point.'

After hearing all this heartening information Josepheos continued, 'A larger team travelling slower and with more stealth will head to Lombrok with the same messages and warning. The remainder of your team will form this group. The rest of the dwarves shall accompany the humans and will travel back to their own homes to spread the news that there may be trouble on its way. All of you should go to Christiana.'

'Now as for all the rest of us, we dragons will stay together, and we will fly north of the route you travelled to get here. We will be travelling to meet up with the sea dragon that is pictured on the Chest. We have not ascertained exactly where he is yet, but we will find him as we fly. I am hoping that Thornfoot and Pria will fly with us, we will carry them on our backs. The rest of the dwarves and humans, travelling in small groups, will return to Christiana, and then on to Ainslia. After your safe arrival home and you have rested you should only then escort the humans to the village of Ainslia. Here they can remain safely until we arrive. This village is on the Great South Sea which is the home of Thesso. This is where we hope we will find him waiting for us.'

Thornfoot went off to talk with Hegal and Elkfast. Hegal had strong leadership skills, and he was courageous, he was also one of the highest ranked members of their group and thus it was fitting that he be the one to communicate all these things to the King. Thornfoot had chosen Elkfast as he knew he was a wise and spirited dwarf with great common sense and would work well with Hegel. Elkfast also had full knowledge of everything going on here inside the cavern and in the city of Cam if the King enquired. He instructed them as to their mission and told them to get ready and set off at speed. He also informed them of the plan to get them quickly on their way, Pria would be waiting outside the wall in the forest directly across from the opening in the wall. Pria, along with Elkfast, knew exactly where that was as they delivered news to each other every day at this spot. She would bring horses from the King Elgrade's personal stable for them. As soon as they were ready to go, he saw them off at the wall of rock. They slipped through the tiny entrance under the wall and disappeared effortlessly into the surrounding forest. He knew they would travel as fast as they could, but he also knew they would stay invisible and was confident they would make the journey home in one piece.

While Thornfoot was getting his teams sorted out Josepheos talked to his oldest and most loyal human servant, 'Therron, I am trusting you to inform and instruct the rest of the humans. You must explain only enough that they understand the plan. They will not all be travelling together, four or five in one group accompanied by the same number of dwarves. Speak with Thornfoot as to setting up the groups. Try to put groups of servants with the same capabilities to travel, together. Make sure that those less fit are provided with helpers along the way. Appoint a leader for each group. You will all be under the authority of the dwarves on this journey and should pay heed to their instructions as they have already travelled this route and know it better than we do. Once in Ainslia you should meet with the Elders. You must meet with a young man called Tarkin. Do not mention this name to anyone until you get there. Not even the dwarves that lead, nor any human. If you meet any other species along the way keep this name to yourself. Along the way do as the leading dwarf instructs. I expect if you happen to meet any one or be questioned regarding your destination, they will have a plan to explain such a group of travellers as yourselves and will be able to provide answers regarding where and why you are travelling together.'

'As soon as we have cleared our prison and are in the air, we will seek out Thesso. When we connect with him, we will show him what is happening here and all that has happened since the Chest has been disturbed. Thesso may have already sensed this energy change so will be seeking answers himself.'

Josepheos turned to his life partner Shari and said, 'Now we must prepare ourselves as well my love. First it will be necessary for us to find our Howdahs. You and I, Shari will have grown so much over the years that I doubt ours will fit us anymore. Miram does not have one, so we will hand ours down. You can give yours to her and take mine, I am confident it will fit you with room to spare,' Josepheos was smiling at Shari when he said this, he did not want her to think he thought she was getting too big. I will have the servants make a new one for me.'

Thornfoot had been listening intently, and now he felt alarmed. He was to ride a dragon! He had no idea what a Howdah was, but he hoped it was a good thing. He hoped it would help him stay on board the dragon. It would. A Howdah is a seat that is strapped onto the back of a dragon or any extremely large beast that another being may wish to ride on. Usually, it is made of leather and woven reeds, and large enough for three or four beings of medium size to sit inside. Dwarf sized passengers would allow more to fit onboard. There are sides on the Howdah and seats on the inside, there are also straps to hang onto and to tie luggage and other stored items down. When using a Howdah in battle the straps are used to strap the occupants inside, so that when the dragon is diving or fighting another dragon the occupants do not fall out. The Howdah is strapped on the back of the dragon just forward of his or her wings. This is the most stable part of the dragon when flying and being in front of the wings gives the occupants more vision to see around about them. Thornfoot thought he would be strapping himself in, for sure. He wondered if he would have the courage to look around at all. His heart was beating a little too fast already, and he was still on the ground.

The servants got to work immediately, sending messages to the surface for the supplies, disguising the needs into smaller different lists over the day so that there would not be any alarms raised by any unusual requests. It was a huge task, and everyone was asked to get involved to ensure the lack of the saddle would not hold the escape attempt up.

As the dwarf teams continued to work on the wall and therefore, creating an escape route for the dragons the humans and dwarves, that could be spared, were sent off to Christiana in small groups. Always they left late at night and stealthily dissolved into the darkness. As the digging and excavation progressed most of the dwarves and humans had escaped. Finally, the Howdah for Josepheos was completed and the Howdahs were fitted to the dragons. It was time to break through the rock veneer that was left concealing the cavern and the excavations taking place behind it. Everyone that was not necessary was gone. Thornfoot and Pria were ready to mount their dragons, and it had been decided at the last minute that the remaining excavators would also ride out of the cavern. Thornfoot would ride on Josephus so that, if necessary, the two could communicate. Pria, along with the diggers, would ride with Shari. Miram would take the last of the diggers. Miriam was so proud of herself. She had never worn a saddle before and now she would have the honour and responsibility of carrying of their rescuers.

During the days as the last dwarfs continued to dig, the preparations within the cavern never stopped. Servants packed food and clothing to be carried by the dragons. Any extra provisions of any kind had been carefully stored and packed up for the road ahead. These would be distributed across the three dragons, according to their capacity to carry, and then tied down inside the three Howdahs, carefully secured and well balanced.

When the wall of rock was ready to be destroyed, they waited a couple of extra nights for a cloudy night. They waited till late in the night, but not too late so that everything would be silent, as the wall would make a noise as it crashed to the ground and the sound of the Dragons' wings would be noisy as well. No one would recognise the sound but after a while they would come out to look around. If they did it when the inns were closing, and businesses were shutting down and workers heading for home it may take more time for them to realise that they had not heard that noise before. Thornfoot and Pria mounted their dragons via rope ladders which would be pulled up into the Howdah after everyone was onboard. The diggers knocked out the bottom layers of rocks and the walls began to crumble. The dwarves scrambled up the ladders as the dragons crouched low on their hind legs waiting to push upward and into freedom. There was no time for hesitation now.

PART THREE

WAR WITH KING ELGRADE AND THE CITY OF CAM

When King Elgrade discovered his prized dragons had been set free, escaped, or stolen. He had no idea which it was but suspected all three, and he was furious. He was shouting at his advisors. His face was red, and his eyes were popping out. He was shouting so loudly and so fast that he was spitting at them as he spoke. The scene was both terrifying and somehow ridiculous. 'His dragons! His, dragons have somehow disappeared from their underground captivity. 'How? When did this happen?' he spat the words vehemently at the confused advisors as they too had no clue as to what had happened. 'How come the alarm was only raised after the food preparers realised food was not being taken from the elevators, and this after two days? What the hell is wrong with you people? Do you have any brains? Heads will roll for this.' He screamed on and on.

'Three large dragons. Three! And fifteen servants do not disappear without a trace, noise, or disturbance. They do not simply vanish. A huge gap in a solid stone wall does not appear overnight. Find out who did this, were they stolen, were they helped, all this right under our feet? And our noses' He blustered, his frustration and anger almost making him incoherent. 'Do I have an army? Are they brainless? Is my security useless? Well, I believe it is. You, my personal advisors have lost my trust completely. You have this day to explain to me how this happened. If you bring me the culprits you may, and I say may, be spared being locked in the cavern yourselves. Send a team to find those who may still be on foot and close to the city. Where are my citizens, have they been taken as well. Eaten maybe. Who can tell. Get men out in pursuit before the hour is up. And when you find anyone involved bring them to me in one piece.'

After this elaborate and noisy outburst King Elgrade hastened the men out of his chambers. He had someone else to consult with. Someone who he kept secret, and someone who he knew would have better results than his councillors. King Elgrade had, for years used the services of a scryer. He did not like others knowing this as he liked them to think that his knowledge came from his own efforts. Having this information made him the strong and he appeared to be the all-knowing one. The scryer did his bidding. Never offering her services to others. For this secrecy and loyalty, he rewarded her well. She lived within the castle and had every luxury at her disposal. King Elgrade had concubines, as far as anyone cared she was just one more. She was not a concubine and the thought of taking her this way made the King quake. He sent for her know and she came at haste.

As he sat waiting King Elgrade considered the dragons and his past actions. He remembered his deal with the dragons and how he had broken his own word. Decades before today a former King Elgrade had imprisoned the dragons out of fear, fear fed to him by the advisors of the day. King Elgrade had led an extraordinarily long life and when his son took over, he enjoyed this same longevity. No one really understood why. He had never changed the dragons' situation.

The three dragons held the answer to all the Kings' longevity. When dragons first came to the city of Cam, they had come here to seek King Elgrade's help. They were fighting a battle to keep their breeding grounds on Kriea Mountain, free from inhabitants. The King agreed to help them, and he did. In exchange for this a pair of dragons would always be stationed in the city and the city of Cam, safe under the protection of these mighty beasts, prospered.

One of King Elgrade's advisors learnt that the dragons had an extremely long life, and he wanted to experiment with the idea that this could be transferred to humans who in comparison had a truly short span of years. He set about taking samples of blood and imbibing it and making up all sorts of experiments trying to learn the secret. It consumed his waking hours, and he became obsessed. He convinced the king that the dragons were not cooperating and were laughing at all the humans. To see what was causing all the upset with his advisor the king held a private audience with the dragons, they told him that there was not any secret as to their long life. They were creatures of magic, and as such did not deteriorate as other creatures did. They did not grow older nor show signs of age because they were not genetically made the way most species were made. They did however grant the King a boon, or a prize, this was in the form of a dragon's disc, it was to be crushed and ground to a fine powder, placed in water and drank sparingly over a long time. Three drops were enough each year to stave of aging. It could not give you eternal life but would slow down your aging process. They warned the King that he should not discuss this with anyone and that the scale was only effective if it was freely given to the user. It could not be harvested or shared.

He kept his word and kept the information to himself, and he kept the powder to himself as well. Those who noticed his appearance tried to get him to reveal what the dragons had told him. Eventually the old King decided to place the dragons in the cavern for their own safety at first, and later as he listened to the words of those who hated the Dragons, he imprisoned them. His word was broken, and the dragons no longer trusted him nor felt they were under any obligation to honour their agreement or remain within the city. Now with their escape the present King Elgrade feared they would find a way home, and what if that led to a dragon uprising against the city. The three dragons had to be found and stopped before they got out of his realm.

The woman came into the room at the King's summons. She was beautiful and King Elgrade wondered again as to why she was not one of his lovers. He dismissed these thoughts as distractions he did not need. He realised that she was too important for that luxury. Her skills were of different nature. Dressed in a bright red robe that fell to the floor she glided into the room. Her chestnut hair was piled up on the top of her head, long ringlets cascaded down her back. Her luminous green eyes seemed to sparkle with an artificial light. She spoke softly to the King, asking his desire. Her lips were soft and pink without a trace of any dye or colouring. The King always found the first sight of her a little overwhelming. She had looked this way for as long as he remembered, he always suspected she was of Elfin blood but did not ask and she did not disclose anything regarding herself. He nervously cleared his throat and regathered his senses before he spoke. She knew of the dragon's captivity and indeed often scried the caves for the King to check on them. He told her of the dragons escape and the implications of this event. He had no idea how they had escaped and asked her to see what had happened and where they were right now.

Aurora began to assemble her tools, first she placed a red cloth on a low table which was only a short distance from the floor. Next a highly decorative bowl was set upon the table. The bowl's surface was inscribed with a series of symbols running all the way around the circumference, it was large and squat and provided a wide surface area. Then, she took a small decorative flask, that she had brought into the room with her and poured an oily liquid into the bowl, filling it to the top. From a deep red velvet bag, she took out seven gemstones and laid these around the bowl. Everything she did she did with purpose. As she placed items, she became sleepier, her eyes became glazed, and they lost focus on the room around her. No longer aware of the King she sat on the richly carpeted floor and gazed into the bowl.

Aurora began to chant softly, a series of repetitious noises, and she began to speak. The King stared into the bowl and saw only the surface, but he listened eagerly to Aurora's voice. 'I see three dragons with Howdahs on their backs. They are being ridden by a selection of small beings that I believe to be dwarves. There are more than three of the riders, it is hard to see into the Howdahs and they are small, but there are possible as many as ten dwarves. There are male and female dwarves present. They are dressed and packed for travel, so this has been a well-planned expedition and carefully prepared for. I cannot place where they are for the sky is clear and they are high above the clouds. I perceive their direction to be easterly and they are travelling at a good speed. That is all I see.' She began to come out of her trance like state.

'Easterly,' Elgrade pondered as to what was to the East. 'Not much between here and the great Eastern Ocean?' thought King Elgrade. 'The Dwarf city of Christiana is toward the East and there is that blasted Den Dargo Forest, full of all sorts of weird things.'

'They must be heading for the underground city. That is good enough for me.' He gritted his teeth with his next words. 'We will start our search there.' He said as he bade Aurora to leave him. She quietly packed up her tools and slid out of the room on silent feet, without speaking another word.

The King contemplated his next move. Rushing headlong into a war with a clan of Dwarves was not to be taken lightly and should be considered a last resort, taken only when all else failed. The last war between the two species had been long and bitter and the humans had not come out without serious loss. A necessary truce had been formed as neither group could gain the upper hand, and concessions had been made on both sides. The truce had held for a long time, and he would be foolish to overlook this fact. But better a Dwarf War than a Dragon War. How to avoid either and retain his Dragons, this was the question he could not answer.

The King decided to send an emissary to the Kingdom of Christiana and ask for an audience with King Paelion. The emissary would also deliver a message from King Elgrade directly to the Dwarf King. Elgrade called his military advisor and asked him to respond with haste.

The Military advisor whose name was Jakovyr came at a trot. Jakovyr was a fine specimen of a man, fit and strong and oozed confidence. He was a supporter of King Elgrade and for this the King was grateful. He could trust Jakovyr although he was not as confident regarding all his advisors. King Elgrade asked Jakovyr directly, as to the location of the Kingdom's outer most troops, and particularly those to the far east of Cam. Jakovyr answered in the positive and it was ascertained that there was a squadron out near the Lombrok River. 'Send a messenger as speedily as you can with a message for King Paelion of Christiana. Use your fastest carrier pigeon to get the message to our outpost. They can then deliver my request personally to King Paelion. I hope to beat those dragons to him. Get everything organised with speed and I will dictate the message for you. As you leave send in my scribe.

King Elgrade dictated his message, and the scribe carefully copied it down on the parchment. It had to be a truly short and precise. The nervous scribe then left the room. Sometime later Jakovyr returned with a beautiful, strong looking, bird. The anxious King tied the message tube to its leg and released him, sending him on his way with the words, 'Go with speed.' The freed bird caught a wind draught and rose rapidly, it is wings already beating hard and its direction turning to the East.

Calling all his council to join him and Jakovyr, the King addressed them with urgency in his voice. 'I have called you here in relation to the catastrophic events of the last few days. None of you has proved to be of any value in finding my dragons or even discovered how they escaped. Apart from a great hole in the wall of the caverns, which we can all see clearly, there is not a thing to go on. Thankfully for all of you and the kingdom, I have other, more reliable ways to find them. They are, as we speak, heading for the Eastern Dwarf Kingdom of Christiana. They are being directed by a team of dwarfs which supports my prediction of their destination.' These dwarves must have helped them to escape, and now are riding away with them.

'I am seeking an audience with King Paelion to see if there is a way to negotiate out of this situation. We have a Squadron in that area, so when we receive word from Paelion that he is willing to receive my delegation, I will send them in to negotiate for us. We may be able to achieve something, to come to an agreement, but I do not think so. I have sent a carrier pigeon to my squadron, informing them of what has happened here. They will be ready for any sign of movement of troops around and out of the area, I am not under any illusion that the King will give my messengers an audience and simply hand over my dragons, as he has gone to a great deal of skullduggery to acquire them.'

Even as the doves beat their wings to leave the city Elgrade was changing his mind. 'I fear we will have to fight to retrieve them. If we do not retrieve the dragons, dead or alive, we will be plunged into war with the Dragon Kingdom. I prefer to fight dwarves!' He was becoming increasingly agitated as he shouted, 'Plan for war, we will march to Christiana as soon as you are ready. Make haste, they will not know we are coming until the dragons arrive, but the beasts are already ahead of us. So, war it will be. We must hit fast and hit hard as I cannot afford a long and drawn-out siege.' He drew a deep breath, 'Bring the war beasts, we will need them to penetrate the caves. I will address the men before we go. You have three days! Two is better'!

While the King of Cam was preparing for war, the dwarves and dragons were making haste across the sky towards the East. Their first destination was not Christiana as King Elgrade had assumed. They were heading directly for the Eastern Ocean and the Great Sea Dragon Thesso.

FINDING THESSO

Thesso lay on the bottom of the ocean, comfortably stretched out along the soft sand on the ocean bed. He may have appeared relaxed but in fact he was not. He observed the world above the surface. He watched the energy in the water as the suns light split the surface of the water into a million diamonds, each flashing light in a myriad of colours. It was such a peaceful scene; it evoked a sense of beauty and calm. But something was not right and despite the serenity of his surroundings he felt a foreboding energy that pressed through the silence.

It was this feeling that stirred him from his meditations and observations. He forced himself to become fully aware and rose to the surface. He expanded his consciousness to find what was causing this uneasy feeling. He tried to get a hold of a thread of anything unusual. He sought out Tarkin, and as usual Tarkin was already connected to his mind. 'I feel it too,' he responded. They combined their minds, concentrated their thoughts, and expanded the field of consciousness together. Then they recognised the energy. An energy as unpleasant as it was unexpected, filled their senses. Hunti!

Thesso was mentally discussing this unwelcome news with Tarkin when a more welcoming presence pushed its way into his mind. Dragons, and they were seeking him, trying to contact him. It had been years since he had heard the voice or mind of Josepheos, but he recognised him immediately and he flooded his mind with an immense feeling of joy and power. Josepheos felt the energy and immediately responded.

'Ah there you are Thesso, it is a joy to connect with you once more, your mind is a delight to mine. My partner Shari and daughter Miriam are here also. May they join the conversation?' Thesso responded with an expression of open joy and opened his mind to the females. 'There are dwarves with you, unusual travelling companions for dragons.' 'Yes,' responded Josepheos, 'and you are not alone either.'

'You are sensing Tarkin, he is the human that I am bound with, it is a long story but to trust me is to trust him, he is part dragon and in return I am part human.' Thesso allowed him to see Tarkin and Tarkin responded to meeting the three dragons with an unrestrained excitement. Thesso continued. 'I will reveal all in time, but I sense some urgency in you so let me discover why you are on your way to me ferrying a group of dwarves.'

Josepheos opened his memories to Thesso and Tarkin and showed them the events of the last few weeks. Thesso, was alarmed at the discovery of the Chest and equally delighted and amazed at the tenacity of the dwarves, and happy to see the dragons freed, all at the same time. Josepheos also revealed the location of the Chest in the City of Christiana. All of them had felt Thesso's alarm when he heard that the Chest had been dug up. Tarkin had reacted as well so Thesso quickly reassured the dragons that it would not be possible for anyone to gain access to the Chest's contents without the cooperation of both himself and Tarkin. They had been taken by surprise, they had felt the Hunti just recently and had felt slight changes in the energy fields around them, now they knew why.

Tarkin shared a vision with the dragons of his desperate ride up the mountain years ago, His intention to cast the Chest into an actively erupting volcano. He allowed them to see the work of the Hunti, and said, 'this invisible energy will be our main enemy in the race to attain the Chest and protect it. There will be others. We have already felt the stirring of the Hunti.'

Josepheos said, 'We have almost arrived at the village of Ainslia where the Volcano is located, the Dwarf city of Christiana is located underground close to the volcano, and it was them who found the Chest. We are being pursued as we speak by the King of Cam who as you know thinks that he owns us dragons. Doubtlessly there are other beings that would be interested in locating this Chest in particular. Can you come into the shore so we can meet, and we can include the dwarfs in the conversation, they are already good at speaking dragon.' He laughed at his own words knowing full well it was the dragons themselves allowing the dwarfs to understand them.'

'Tarkin is already in Ainslia, and I will come into the shore immediately, how far away are you? Thesso enquired of Josepheos. 'We will arrive on the shore by tomorrow morning. Can you be there then?' Josepheos asked. Tarkin and Thesso spoke in unison, 'We will be there.' Thesso had already decided that once the three dragons, along with Tarkin and the dwarves had conversed he would ask one of the dragons and Thornfoot to return to Christiana to retrieve the Chest and bring it to him here in Ainslia.

Thornfoot did not know exactly what was being shared between the Sea Dragon and Josepheos, but he knew that the result had been satisfactory to Josepheos. He asked Josepheos what had transpired and Josepheos told him all that was said. The dwarf was relieved, and he was also a little anxious. He hoped the Great Sea Dragon would not be angry at their discovery of the Chest and the course of events that discovery had instigated. There was no point worrying about this, so he turned his thoughts to the others who had escaped the caverns, and where they were now. He wondered aloud to Josepheos as to their fate and when the groups with the humans would arrive in Ainslia.

Hegal and Elkfast with the aid of their horses, and the fact they had left five days before the final wall came down, had already arrived in Christiana. They had experienced no interruptions to their travel. They had informed King Paelion of what had transpired in Cam. Also telling him of how the others planned to retreat and return home and that the dragons themselves with Thornfoot and Pria on their backs, were on the way to find Thesso. They believed he would be in the Eastern Ocean and that is where they were heading. After the dragons had talked with Thesso and received his directions as to what to do with the Chest they would come to Christiana.

The dragons had impressed on Hegal to inform King Paelion that the King of Cam would not take the loss of the dragons lightly and would be on his way to attempt to recover them as soon as he established the connection between the dwarves and their escape. The two had made such haste that they made the risky decision to go by the city of Joannamere to warn King Lombrok that the Cam army may march his way as well. Lombrok did not think they would come to his city as any entrance to Joannamere was well disguised, and he felt the King would bypass it and head for the more well-known dwarf City of Christiana. They had also asked for King Lombrok to prepare his troops as they felt That King Paelion would need them. King Elgrade would be determined to retrieve the Dragons and therefore he would be a fierce enemy. Hegal also informed him that when his dwarves left the caverns in Cam to return home that they would be travelling with humans. They understood that the humans would be accompanied to the village of Ainslia, but their speed would depend on how they were able to travel. After this detour they made haste for Christiana. Now the two men, with their immediate mission accomplished, excitedly headed home to the welcome of their families, for a bath and home cooked meal.

The two larger groups of dwarf diggers that had joined them from Joannamere, to help with the excavation of the caverns, had returned home and King Lombrok was immediately updated of what had happened at Cam. King Lombrok listened intently stroking his chin, now and again, his eyes widening in surprise. When they had finished with their story, he thanked them for their work and told them to go to their families for a well-earned rest.

LOMBROK
PREPARES HIS ARMY

King Lombrok urgently called his advisors, and as soon as they were assembled, without any formalities he addressed them, 'Well dear clansmen and women, I am not at all sure how the dwarves pulled off this escape or rescue really, I do not know how it was orchestrated. How did they manage to pull this off? I sent our teams in because of the request from King Paelion. I expected they would return home after realizing the task was impossible, but I have been surprised and now we have a serious situation on our hands. Cam will not take the loss of the dragons lightly, I can see Elgrade now, hopping up and down screaming. His damaged pride and rage will not abate until he has those dragons back in Cam. He will be preparing for war.'

'How ready are we? I do not believe it necessary to state that we will support King Paelion and Christiana. It is not only my duty, and yours to do so but our honour as well. Make sure we are ready. Get the men and women together and prepare for what every comes our way. Make sure our siege chambers are ready. Fill them with sufficient supplies for a long wait. Start moving the children, old, infirm and those not prepared for the battlefield into the chambers. When the time comes the doors can be sealed. If we are prepared, there will be no delay when called upon and we can march when needed.'

'Send scouts to Cam and see what Elgrade is doing. Do not interfere or engage. Stealth it is, for now. Also send a messenger to Cristiana to inform King Paelion and the Clan Elan of our loyalty, that we are preparing for battle, and we await his call.'

After this long speech King Lombrok sent all out except his military. He addressed them separately and urgently, 'Men get ready, be prepared to march on my order. I do not understand what exactly the situation is, nor do I know what is in the Chest, the Chest that has started all this upheaval, therefore I do not know what it is we fight or. Whatever it is the importance is significant, something is of such import that a team of dwarves have broken into the caverns under Cam. They risked their lives to get to the caves and find the dragons. Whatever it is they asked of them the dragons have responded. The dragons have left the caverns with the dwarves and fly even now to the East. This is after two hundred years of patience. They risk war and their own death to protect this one Chest. A cause of such importance cannot be stood aside from. We will stand with the dragons and with Christiana!'

TRAVELLING HOME

Meanwhile the two groups of dwarves and humans were making their way slowly but steadily along, travelling after dusk to not draw attention to themselves. The dwarves had great skills of finding places to conceal oneself during the day and they were able to see very well in the dark. The pace was slow as the humans had not been physically active for years. The confines of the cave giving them little reasons to explore, and they simply did their allotted chores. Most enjoyed being out of the caverns and were happy and gave it their best effort, but it was still a much slower speed to that the dwarves would have preferred.

As they continued their journey the dwarves' shared stories with them about what they had encountered on their way to Cam. They told them of the great dwarf cities under the ground and the humans were amazed, as they had always believed that dwarfs where the characters of fairy tales. The Dwarves also recounted to them details of the more unsettling things they had dealt with on the way. They spoke of the energy that had chased them, and of the creatures in Den Dargo Forest. The humans were wide eyed and not sure what was true and what was not.

It was late afternoon and one of the groups had resumed their travels. Feeling well rested after sleeping during the day they were quite relaxed and contented. Early that morning before Dawn they had passed the entrance to the City of Joannamere. Only the dwarves knew this as it was well disguised. They were now only a short distance from Den Dargo, and they hoped to reach its outskirts by the evening when, out they heard the thunders of hooves. They reacted with speed as they realised, they were being pursued. Myrtle and Treeturn instructed the others to get off the road, they all clamoured into the rocks and clefts that followed the mouth of the Lombrok River where it disappeared underground. The four humans and two dwarves concealed themselves and not long after the riders pounded past their hiding place. Stay very still Myrtle whispered to the group. 'They will be back when they realise that they have lost our tracks.'

Night fell around them and darkened the crevasses where they lay hidden. The horses were returning when Myrtle felt a soft touch on her shoulder, alarmed she looked up, peering into the darkness she gazed into the large, illuminous eyes of a creature she had never seen before. 'I will help you, lay still and wait for me to return. I must take care of the horses and men that are pursuing you so that you can pass.' Whispered the little creature. Myrtle turned to Treeturn with a questioning look, 'What do you think?' her expression implied. Treeturn nodded his head. 'Yes.' He had heard the tiny creature as well.

Myrtle realized with a start that the creature had not spoken to her at all, but she had heard the message loud and clear. The rest of her party froze in place at Myrtle's signal. She had no idea what she had seen nor how it could possible do anything to the horses, but she felt she compelled by the small creature to take it at its word. They waited remaining still and quiet.

Myrtle took this time to concentrate of their helper. She felt rather than saw that this was a female before her. Three sets of short wings flapped continuously seeming to anchor the little one in place. She had bright luminous eyes that seemed too big for her head. Her skin was pale blue and appeared to be soft like fine fur. Six limbs came out of the torso in front of the wings. Myrtle was not sure if they were legs or arms but felt they must fulfil both functions as no other limbs were seen. Her body was long and thin, about twice the size of her head and torso. It resembled a leg, as it had a larger part at the bottom, but it was not a at all like foot.

Watching Myrtles observation of herself the creature spoke again. 'I am a Tranzicon, my home world is Tranzia. My name is Minna, and this is Tomas,' she motioned over her shoulder with one of her appendages and then continued talking. 'Tomas will go now as he will lead our army. We have been here on this planet since the movement between worlds failed centuries ago. We inhabit the Den Dargo which is just ahead of us. The noise of the riders alerted us to your danger, so we came out to help. We remembered your group passing through the forest weeks ago.' 'Do you remember us? We saw you in Den Dargo, but I do not think you realised we were there as we kept to our woven homes deep in the reeds and swamps. We did fly alongside you for a time so we could learn what we could about your species. We also felt the energy of the unseen enemy that was pursuing you, it did not seem interested in us at all. We went as far as we could and returned to the forest. Do you know what the source of that frightening energy was?'

Myrtle gave a bit of a shudder as she remembered the silent, invisible, menace chasing them, and then she smiled as she thought of their loud singing and hurried walking. 'We don't know,' she said. 'We have not encountered it again.' 'I have recorded what I can of them, and I am happy to share this information with you.' 'Have any other groups like us passed this way?'

The little Tranzicon told her. 'Yes, one group came through the evening before this one. They were happy and travelling steadily toward Ainslia.' Mrytle was relieved to hear this, and she wondered aloud to Treeturn and the others where everyone else was.

Minna began to talk to her again, 'As we speak you can hear the horses, they are under attack from our army. Yes, Tomas has led out our army. Do not be concerned we are well equipped to upset a horse.' She smiled mischievously as she showed Myrtle a large spike that had suddenly appeared on the top of her head. Myrtle could hear the horses as they screamed and whinnied and the men shouted and yelled, eventually the horses fled, and she could no longer hear them. The men, cursing and shouting after the horses, finally gave up, and they could hear them running after the horses in the direction that they had come from minutes earlier. Waiting a little longer the group squeezed out of their cracks and crannies, there were yelps of pain as bones not used to exercise creaked as they got to their feet, they thanked their rescuers and agreed to follow them through the forest.

THE DRAGONS ARRIVE IN AINSLIA

Tarkin had addressed the villagers as to the imminent arrival of the three dragons, and that they were not intent on harming anyone. None of the villagers except Tarkin had any memory of the last encounter with the great Sea dragon Thesso, but he was the subject of hundreds of bedtime stories. People often spoke of seeing him out to sea, drifting deep below the surface of the ocean, others swore they had seen him in the shallows talking with Tarkin but overall, he was a mystery to them.

Thesso was now just offshore in Ainslia and was waiting to sight the dragons before he too revealed himself. Tarkin anxiously paced the shoreline. Tarkin sensed Thesso was not far out to sea, so he dove into the water and swam out to meet him. Since Tarkin's miraculous rescue years ago he had been imbued with an extraordinary ability to swim great distances and to stay under the water longer that he should have been able to. Just another thing that made him different to most humans. But Tarkin was not human at all.

Finding Thesso he climbed up onto his back for a thrilling ride to shore. How the people cheered, ran away, panicked, and about turned themselves inside out to get the best view of the great sea dragon. Suddenly, three dragons appeared over the village, sparking excitement and terror. Hearing the words that three dragons will arrive soon and be landing in your village is not at all like the actual arrival of three huge dragons. There was gasping, shouting, and running here and there in panic, excitement, laughter, fear, were all expressed in aways from hundreds of mouths. Babies cried and mothers hushed them, dogs barked furiously from a safe distance and all the other animals fled. Swooping downward, with their dwarf riders holding on tight, the three dragons landed on the beach.

Thornfoot's stomach rose rapidly upwards into his mouth and then descended to his feet at a rapid rate. With an iron will he managed not to vomit. He wondered how Pria was going but as he looked over toward Miriam, he could not see Pria above the walls of the Howdah. He could see the heads of other dwarfs above the top and they were okay, so nothing appeared amiss. Thornfoot climbed out of the Howdah and down the ladder, his feet touched the ground, and they could not hold his weight, and he unceremoniously fell over. His legs were like jelly and unstable, embarrassed he glanced across to where the others were dismounting the dragons. Dwarves were staggering around and falling over everywhere. In the end they all sat on the ground for a good, long moment and laughed and laughed.

By now a huge crowd had gathered, the whole village was on the beach waiting to see what going to happen next. It was an incredulous day.

Thesso with Tarkin still on his head, greeted the dragons as they walked down into the shallows, the dwarves came along. Thesso, Tarkin and Josepheos talked via their mind connections. Miriam and Shari listened with interest. A decision had to be made. Thornfoot was asked for his advice as to the King of Christiana's reaction to learning that he must give up the Chest immediately. 'I do not know; I cannot speak for the King. He is very committed to the protection of his kinsmen. If whatever is in the Chest will harm them, he will surely give it up.' Thesso responded assertively. 'It is not only harmful to them but to all of us.'

Thesso decide to give Thornfoot a timely insight of what was at stake. 'I do not know what you know, or what your legends tell you about a Portal between worlds, time, and space. This is what is in the Chest. Tarkin and I put it in the Chest years ago, we used it for personal reasons but mostly to grow and learn. But the Hunti a powerful force of evil wanted to use it and came to take it from us. Villagers of Ainslia were murdered and others had to flee for their lives. It is a long story that we do not have time to tell. To end any possibility that the Hunti may acquire the Chest, Tarkin bravely fled with it up the volcano, with the Hunti at his feet he managed to throw it into the volcano. That is where you found it. Now that is has been exposed and discussion has been made as to what it is and what it holds the talk has reached the Hunti and they have felt it is available once more and are searching for it. There is not time for any hesitation.'

Are we all agreed, Josepheos and Thornfoot will fly to Christiana, King Paelion will be expecting you since Hegal and Elkfast have returned to update him of the escape. Josepheos and Thornfoot will retrieve the Chest and return to us as fast as possible. Speaking directly to the two he emphasised the dangers. 'Stop for nothing. Call me, if necessary, he said to Josepheos, I think it best if the rest of us stay here together we can discuss further plans and we can protect each other and the village.' Turning to Tarkin he said, 'The dwarves need food and a place to rest. The dragons and I will have a chat. Please stay connected Tarkin, we will need you.'

As Thornfoot reluctantly climbed the rope ladder up to the Howdah on Josepheos' back he had conflicting feelings. He was happy to be getting back to Christiana, and proud to be of service to the great beasts he had helped free, but flying again, well he was not so sure of that. The dragons walked up the beach, Tarkin led the rest of the party to a large hall. Food and wine had been set out and there were pallets set up along the wall. The dwarves had finally got their land legs and eagerly took the food offered to them.

As the lone dragon and dwarf disappeared into the heavens Thesso drew a deep breath. What would this next few weeks cost them all. He thought they had got the Chest where it would never be found, never become exposed, but they had been wrong. This time they had to get it right.

JAKOVYR MAKES READY CAM'S ARMY

With a heavy heart Jakovyr addressed his men. Men he must know prepare for battle. War with the dwarves was always a last resort. He felt king Elgrade had not taken enough time to even see if the negotiators could get him an audience with King Paelion, he was rushing in and that never turned out well. Elgrade wanted the dragons back, but they would not be easily taken and would more likely be taken dead than alive. He hated that thought. Even more than that he hated the thought of fighting the magnificent but powerful creatures. They would have all the advantages, and his men would be burnt, crushed, or would flee in terror. The outcome of this fighting would be death on a catastrophic scale, somehow, he felt losing the dragons would be just as bad as losing his men. He was concerned about this upcoming battle. Also, he was wary of the fact that Elgrade had mercenaries in his armies, and he knew that there was every possibility that they would desert if the battle was too intense. The army was what would stay till the very end and take the brunt of the fighting.

Despite all of this and his personal feelings regarding the dragons, he knew he would honour his King, and he would fight as directed by the King. His compatriots would stand with him. If Death came to call him, he would go. He hoped he would put up a good fight.

Preparing the war beasts was another story entirely and after addressing his men and telling them to be ready to march on the third day, he walked around the city to where he knew the handlers would be preparing the beasts. The noise greeted him first and it chilled his blood.

Huge beasts, which looked like elephants but were much bigger, stomped and bellowed as they were fitted out with their war metal. Their huge heads swung wildly, and the keepers nimbly jumped out of the way. Here and there they gave the beasts a sharp smack, but it was not noticed by them. Their skin which was unusually thick was covered in places with huge scales and much of it was now decked out with spikes and chain mail. The huge heads wore helmets of spikes. Just looking at them sent shivers down his spine. Lan wondered if they could be of help with the dragons without killing everyone in their way and that included him and his men.

He spoke directly to Tanir who was the chief handler. Tanir had walked into the city two years ago and had gone to see the animal handlers, he had asked to be employed and now here he was, the head handler to the war beasts. No one had queried where he came from. 'How do you think they will go against the dragons?' Jakovyr asked tentatively. Tanir himself was not a person you wanted to be on the wrong side of. Tall, muscular, and hairy, he stood a couple of feet over Jakovyr's head. He was always snarling at someone or something. Tanir shook his head, 'On the ground they have a good chance of being effective, but in the air the dragons are out of our league. If our Lancers can bring them down or slow them down, well who knows.'

'Personally, I do not want to be within a few leagues of that battle.' He smiled at Jakovyr showing huge teeth that were surprisingly white against his hairy black face. Reaching out, what he thought was a reassuring arm he gave Lan's shoulder a pat, which combined with the wide smile nearly made Jakovyr retreat in terror. 'We'll be in there, Mate, along with the dogs, we'll do some damage for sure.' He said reassuringly, Jakovyr hoped it was damage to the enemies and not to his troops.

After acknowledging Tanir's comment he decided to check out the dogs while he was over this side of the city, he did not want to come back this way soon. The dogs of all shapes and sizes were barking and snapping at his heels, those were the ones out of the cages. 'These are the friendly ones.' yelled Jaques their trainer and handler as he came over too. He had a big smile on his face. He was completely different in appearance that Tanir. A small man with long blonde hair, he was often smiling and could be heard singing around the cages. Dogs were controlled by connection and trust. They wanted to do what the handlers asked of them. If they did not want to do it there was not any force that could make them. 'Thank goodness.' said Jakovyr, 'but I am not so sure of that friendliness.'

'How is your preparation coming on?' He asked. 'We are all ready to go except for upgraded armour that we are waiting for, the older dogs have outgrown their original suits. We have a sizeable number of, surprisingly well-trained, teams of dogs right now. They will be effective if the handlers can hold them.' 'We have a couple of young handlers that are new this season, if the dogs are not completely connected to them, they will never hold them in a battle scenario, then that's when things can get a bit crazy.' He stopped talking, hesitating before continuing, 'I am not sure how they will react to the dragons. Shit scared of them usually so may have to use them elsewhere.' 'I'll remember that!' said Jakovyr, thanking Jaques, he turned away, shaking excited pups off his legs he slowly walked back to his quarters. Tomorrow he would address his men. Then all the garrison leaders would independently address their troops.

THE HUNTI

Jakovyr was beginning to feel an anxiety that was uncommon to
him. He did not like war, but he did not fear it either. He was a
warrior. He lived and died by this. He would do his job as long as he
could, this was no different to other times, he had prepared himself
and his men as he efficiently and as well as he could. The rest was in
the hands of the Gods. Gods in whom he did not believe. This fear
and apprehension were different to any he had felt before. It was like
something unnerving was happening around him and he could not
pinpoint it.

What he was sensing was the Hunti. All the fuss and fear of war
made Cam the perfect place for the Hunti to be. They sucked up the
anger and fear. As usual the Hunti fed on negativity of all sorts. They
loved fear and pain as this energy caused them to expand and divide.
Worry and doubt fed them as well. Any sadness at all made them
grow. But pain was what they were waiting for. A battlefield would be
perfect. They would move with the army.

While the largest party of Hunti had stayed in Cam others, antic-
ipating the fight ahead, had followed the dragons. They sensed the

Chest and the energy it would eventually give them. They were careful keeping themselves outside of the energy fields of the dwarves and the dragons. Or so they thought, but the dragons were aware, they also knew that acknowledging a Hunti gives it power. They kept their reactions between themselves.

Thornfoot had told them of the energy following them on the way to Cam. They felt that this would be the same thing. They remembered a time when the Hunti destroyed the villages and small hamlets in and around the Eastern Ocean. At that time Thesso and his human friend Tarkin had saved the day.

Thornfoot had not felt the Hunti yet, but he was experiencing a wide range of feelings to distract him. He was on a dragon, in the sky. Again! Looking down on the land as if it were a picture laid out before him. He was excited, he was terrified, and he was happy. He also felt quite ill, but all of this was nothing to him. He was flying!

CAM'S ARMY MARCHES

King Elgrade, mounted on his royale steed, was in full regalia. The royal colours of Cam, blue and gold, flew from his banner and his pitch-black horse's headdress. He looked impressive as he addressed his advisors and generals one last time before they marched to Christiana, where they believed they would find the dragons stolen by the dwarf team. They would demand their return and restitution for the act of aggression by the Dwarf Kingdom. If the dwarf King did as he demanded, he may save himself and his city from destruction. Elgrade puffed himself up with these self-righteous thoughts and plans. He rode his magnificent horse ahead of his army through the inner and then the outer gates to the sound of huge cheers. Pipes and drums played, and it was an extremely excited crowd that watched the army's departure. Once out of sight of the city gates Elgrade would retreat to the middle ranks where the Kings guard would surround him.

As the news of the Kings march to war spread, different ethnic groups began to prepare themselves for their part in the battle. There were those who would side with the City of Cam and the and King Elgrade. Others would not be, due to long standing agreements and treaties with different Cities and Species

The Elves were one of the groups that would not stand with Cam for this battle even though this was where they had been given a haven for centuries. They had a much longer standing agreement to fight with and to support all dragon kind. This agreement was so old that none of the elves knew exactly why and when it came into being, but it had been passed down to them and it was now a part of their psyche. There was no questioning this loyalty. The dragons were in danger, and they would defend them with all their strength. The fact that they would have to fight alongside the Dwarf Nations, a group they had no love for, was not enough to change this. They began to pack up their weapons and leave the city, exiting in small groups to avoid attention. They moved with stealth and were unnoticed by the residents of Cam. Quickly and quietly, they began to follow the direction the dragons had taken. They moved with speed and made good ground, it was not long until they could see the dragons high in the sky and flying East.

MANGARA STIRS UP HIS PROPHETS

Mangara, the ancient sorcerer, called his followers to him. In a great flourish of energy, he declared to them that the time he had prophesied for years and years was finally upon them. The Portal he had been seeking for centuries to take them to vast worlds was in his grasp. Worlds beyond their wildest dreams and imagining would be at their feet, money and power would follow. Mangara used his manipulative power to fill his followers' minds with images of their desires, he took away all their doubts and fears. He demonstrated his own powers of illusion and his ability to confuse his enemies with false ideas and thoughts, thus he led them to believe in their own ability to achieve the Portal. They would follow the Hunti to the Portal. Mangara knew the Hunti were already in pursuit of the Portal, and he also knew that they would never surrender the Portal if they acquired it before he did. His only hope was to trick them into allowing him to use it along with them and then somehow to cause enough distraction to leave them somewhere and escape with the Portal. Only then he would be satisfied, and all power would be his.

Mangara knew that the dwarves, along with the Dragons of Cam, and other groups would be looking to destroy the Portal, for the last time, as soon as they could get hold of it. The King of Cam already marched towards them to retrieve his dragons. Although he had no knowledge of the Portal, he would assume his right to it and assume that the might and strength of his army would make it his as soon as he realised what it was and what it could do for his kingdom and for him. He would be intent on having the Portal for himself.

JOSEPHEOS AND THORNFOOT RETRIEVE THE CHEST

Josepheos and Thornfoot reached Christiana and King Paelion in a brief time. The dwarves were expecting them and a large party, mostly warriors were above ground when they first saw the City. Thornfoot indicated where a small clearing was waiting for Josepheos to land, but Josepheos was already diving down towards it. Thornfoot grabbed the sides and swallowed his fear, and his lunch. He tried to be brave and standing up tall as they landed, he greeted his King from the Howdah. Although the dwarves were unsettled and a bit alarmed by the size of the dragon they stood their ground around King Paelion. On seeing Thornfoot climbing out of the Howdah and sliding down the ladder to the ground they gave out a loud cheer. Thornfoot hurried to King Paelion and gave him Thesso's message word for word. There was no doubt in the urgency in Thornfoot voice as he told them of the contents of the Chest.

King Paelion gathered his council, and they all sat down together and quickly discussed what they had heard. Thornfoot was earnest in his desire for haste and reassured them that they had no reason to distrust Thesso and Josepheos. The huge dragon, Josepheos, was napping in the sunlight, readying himself for the flight back to the Eastern Ocean. King Paelion came to a decision and men were sent down the mineshaft to retrieve the Chest. Thornfoot reassured them that there was nothing for them to fear while retrieving and delivering the Chest so they were able to make haste and return as quickly as they could. Even as they waited King Elgrade's army was on its way. King Paelion must prepare for war. He had work to do, and he was happy to see the Chest gone from the city.

Less than an hour later Josepheos stood patiently as Thornfoot, with the Chest in his possession climbed the ladder to the Howdah. Thornfoot had to look brave as now his wife, Therese, was watching, a look of pride combined with love and worry on her face. King Paelion had sent for her so that she and Thornfoot were able to spend a last moment together before he had to leave once more. He had given her one last long hug before he picked up the Chest. At once he climbed into the Howdah, he tied the Chest securely onto the shelf, close to the floor in front of his feet. He shouted out to Josepheos that he was ready to go as he harnessed himself in. He then stood on the bench so he could look over the sides to wave a brave farewell to his beloved wife and to his King and Clansmen.

PAELION GETS READY FOR AN ATTACK ON CHRISTIANA

Almost immediately the dragon was out of sight Paelion called his leaders to prepare the city for war. They had already started preparations with the arrival of Hegal and Elkfast but now that they knew King Elgrade was already on his way, they began to make haste to be ready. Christiana was an underground city; therefore, it could be defended in diverse ways. Past attackers had tried to make tunnels into the city from a strategic position while their main army attacked the entrance. This knowledge was passed on and other armies are aware of this strategy, and they look for preexisting entrances and outlets. Already guards had been set on every existing tunnel so there would be no possibility of a surprise attack this way. The main entrance to the City of Christiana was a cave, purposely quite small, just dwarf head high, it continued back into the earth for about twenty meters in his way, it appeared to end abruptly in a solid wall of stone but there was a concealed turn that opened to a very large cavern. This was a meeting hall and used for events and shows. A thousand dwarfs could fit in the hall and move around and socialise.

Underground within the main city there was a hive of activity going on. The children and babies along with their grandparents and all elderly and infirm where being moved deep into the belly of the city. Narrow passageways, could be defended by a single soldier, led you to these safe chambers. Food and water were being topped up and individual rooms prepared. The dwarfs had not had to take these precautions for years, but they were always ready for the day that they were needed. Most dwarf cities had safe rooms, and these were prepared over time and were well thought out. Though seemingly impenetrable there was always an escape route. There were passageways that would outlet a long way from the city, with a concealed entrance that, in time of war, would be heavily guarded. Other escape routes did not outlet to the surface but travelled a long distance underground and reached other dwarf communities or cavern systems.

As the safe chambers were being filled and organised the warrior groups were preparing for the battle itself. Blacksmiths worked ceaselessly with hammer and tong to sharpen swords and spears. Hammers were made and battle axes sharpened. Shields were hammered out and passed out. While some dwarfs chose to wear full armour, others did not. Full armour can restrict movement; however, most wore a chest plate. Archers checked their bows and arrows, weighing the balance of each, partly to allay nerves and partly to make sure all was as ready to use. The city was a hive of movement and noise, but it was clear that the commotion was well organised.

It was in the huge main cavern that the army was forming up. Rank after rank of warriors, both male and female stood shoulder to shoulder listening to Graynor, King Paelion's Senior Advisor. More troops poured in as they completed their preparation. As he addressed the soldiers he reminded them of their duty. Graynor spoke with a fierce passion and urgency in his voice, said, 'If the King of Cam tries to force us to surrender something of great peril to us all, something that would increase his own power, well he will not find us easily persuaded to give this up. If he wants to recapture the three dragons that he has broken his word and agreement with over a hundred years ago, we are not going to help him achieve that end. If Elgrade wishes to harm our elderly and babies, then he will find you warriors a force to recon with.' He spoke to them of what to expect regarding Elgrade's war beasts. 'Everything that lives can and will die. Do not be afraid of them. Remember we have the dragons and a large force of humans; it is said that Tarkin's kin are Superhuman, and they all fight on our side in this battle. Elgrade's army will be under attack from all sides. So, fight bravely, hold your ground and fight for your family, your clan, and your honour.' He went on and reminded them of their Clan brothers in Joannamere, 'King Lombrok awaits our summons and direction to assist us in this battle. He is family and he and his fighters are steadfast in battle. We do not go to this battle out matched by the Cam army.'

After this rousing speech by Graynor, King Paelion himself, surrounded by his personal guard addressed them all, walking through the ranks, he spoke to them personally. Moon Ray, walking with him, did the same. Then the King made his way to the front of the gathered soldiers and gave a last encouraging word, he spoke passionately and emotionally, 'My Personal guard will be in the fight with you, as will I, do not doubt we will stay with you whatever the outcome,' King Paelion stood in front of the warriors, he raised his arm to the sky, his fist was clenched in a triumphant salute. Patriotism and determination filled the hearts of the warriors and fear was pushed aside.

ASSEMBLY IN AINSLIA

It was an eclectic group that had gathering on the shore of the Eastern Ocean near the small village of Ainslia. Never had such an army been assembled.

The last of the humans had arrived in Ainslia with their dwarf escorts. The humans were taken to the village and given over to their fellow humans to be cared for. Most had improved in health during the long walk and apart from being tired, were keen to join the forces preparing to fight. The dwarf escort was eager to tell the leaders what had happened and about their saviours in the Den Dargo Forest. Myrtle had recorded all she had learned about the Tranzicons, how they were willing to help the dragons, and she assured them that despite their tiny stature they would be fierce allies. She recalled to Thesso, Tarkin and the other dragons how they had been able to disrupt the horses and send them running in all directions. Shari was excited to hear this as she had been fearful of what the huge war beasts would bring to the battle and feared for the smaller dwarves in their path. Even the dogs could be disrupted. This was a good development.

The elves had started to arrive in numbers in Ainslia and were reporting immediately to the dragons for updates and instructions. The dragons were thrilled to see the elves and humbled to see that even though, at this point the dragons numbered only four, the elves still honoured the ancient agreement. The elves were able to give an update on the size and makeup of the Cam army. They confirmed that the mammoth like war beasts were marching with the army, and a squadron of dogs and trainers were also on the way. When they had last seen the army, it was marching at fast pace to Christiana, as Elgrade believed that the dragons had been taken there, and that King Paelion wanted to keep the dragons for himself.

Tarkin's family began to arrive from near and far, a group of super humans ready to fight for their beliefs. Over the years the family had increased in numbers and hundreds of men and women marched up the beach to join the dragons. They believed in the freedom of the dragons, and feeling the passion of their ancestor Tarkin, they wanted the Hunti stopped in their tracks. They also intended to stop the Portal falling into the wrong hands.

There were also the villagers of Ainslia, they were preparing to fight and making weapons as they could. They were all farmers, but they would stand up when the time came. Food and grain were being harvested and brought in from the fields, to save it from destruction and to feed the hungry fighters gathering on the shore. Men and women filled the huge halls that had been quickly erected on the beach to provide cooking and eating areas. People moved around creating meals and serving them others kept everything clean and tidy.

To add to this powerful force the dragons from Kriea had been summoned to see if any could assist. Messages had also been, and were constantly being sent, to all air dragons to assist as soon as possible.

It was into this scene Thornfoot and Josepheos arrived back at the village. They landed in the shallow water as Thesso rose out of the sea to greet them. 'Do you have the Chest he bellowed,' for all to hear. He knew they did because he had been in mind contact with Josepheos the whole journey, but he wanted all the others on the beach to know that they had been successful in the first phase of the plan.

HIDING THE CHEST AND REPELLING THE HUNTI

Now to get the Chest into a safe location, Thesso's plan was to take the Chest and drop it far out to sea. there was a deep trench about two hundred miles from the shore. It was formed when the earth itself was forming. The movement of the Tectonic plates caused rifts sometimes up to ten thousand meters deep. Thesso had never reached the bottom of this one, so he did not know how deep, but it was deep enough. At this depth, the ocean has no oxygen, and few creatures moved and lived, those that did had adapted themselves to see in pitch blackness and to absorb the chemicals available in the water. They adapted to high pressures and low temperature. The movement of the plates was continuous. As a place to live it was not inviting but as a hiding place it was perfect.

This was not Thesso's first plan, he had thought to open the Chest and reabsorb the Portal into his own body, but he was not sure this would stop those wanting the Portal from killing him in their attempts to control it. If this happened, he and Tarkin would die. The rest of the village and indeed the world of Pardow would be left helpless in the face of the Hunti, and a bloodbath of alarming proportions would ensue. No, it had to be taken where there was no access. He had discussed this with Tarkin, and they agreed that the Hunti had not been able to follow them out into the water previously, and, as they believed the Hunti to be the only ones hunting the Portal, it made good sense to use the ocean to hide it once more. Taking everything into consideration, along with the need for haste, using the trench was a good plan.

They both hoped that this time they had made the correct decision. Years ago, they had hidden it in fire but over a hundred years later, a dead volcano and a clan of dwarfs had unearthed it. They silently hoped water was the answer.

Calling Tarkin to bring the Chest and to climb up onto his neck for the trip out to sea Thesso tasked Josepheos to remain on high alert and to control the situation here on the beach. He and Tarkin disappeared into the ocean. Thesso was already mind talking the Tarkin as he slipped under the water and dove down into the ocean, 'We can travel faster if we stay underwater, I know you think you cannot do this, but the truth is you can. Just relax and breathe as normal. It is time you learnt another of your talents,' Tarkin trusted Thesso so he agreed to try and did as he was instructed, he was delighted when he realised that he could breathe under water. On the way to the trench Thesso sent out a summons to all the sea dragons in the Eastern Sea to come to the shore, he allowed them to read his mind giving them information and pictures of the battle in Ainslia and asking them to be ready to support anyone fleeing into the ocean. The elderly citizens and the children and babies of Ainslia were already in boats heading out to sea and he wanted them to be protected from the elements and anything else that may attempt to harm them. The boats were to be directed to the same island that had provided refuge years before.

The Hunti force had grown in numbers and were impatiently awaiting the arrival of the Portal, they had not realised immediately that it was being transferred to Thesso. When they saw that Tarkin was carrying the Chest with the Portal inside towards the shore, and Thesso they were furious and began to attack those on the beach. But Thesso was already under the water. They could not follow Thesso and Tarkin because the air over the ocean with its increased humidity and salt spray changed the energy in which they moved. They could not penetrate the ocean surface, so they turned on the Elves and Dragons with a vicious attack. At first it was mayhem as no one could see the enemy, but they could feel them.

Josepheos called everyone to get behind him and Shari, they intended to use fire against the Hunti. Miriam having been sent to warn and protect the villagers was not with them. Tarkin's family moved forward to stand beside the dragon, and they too directed fire at the attacking force. The dragons were emitting fireballs from their huge mouths and the men were pouring flames from their outstretched fingertips. What a sight it made. As the fire hit the Hunti they were forced to move back, here and there they simply exploded as the energy around them changed and gases in the air released compounds that they could not control. As soon as their shapes were revealed in the smoke and fog the elves were able to use their bows.

Fighting a losing battle the Hunti decided to retreat. They moved to attack the village of Ainslia, but Miriam was waiting, she began to breathe fire in their direction, the Hunti, caught between her and the other dragons who were now chasing them across the beach and running towards her, turned and fled. As anger and frustration filled them, the Hunti retreated the way that they had come and sought out the army of King Elgrade on which they would release their fury.

King Elgrade was marching with speed to Christiana when he received, not one, but two carrier Pidgeon messages. The first told him to avoid the Enchanted Forest, or as it was sometimes called, Den Dargo. The message was to inform him that in this forest an unseen enemy had attacked his men. Their horses had been driven crazy by this invisible force and had fled the scene, leaving their riders to be attacked mercilessly. They had run all the way back to Cam, never overtaking or sighting their mounts. The second message was of much more importance as it informed him that the dragons he considered to belong to him, were not at the Dwarf City of Christiana but had flown on to the Eastern Ocean close to the village of Ainslia and having landed on the beach were met by a large sea serpent.

Poor Elgrade had no idea of what, or who, a sea serpent was, but he did not imagine it was a huge ocean-going dragon. He stopped the Army. They ceased their march forward while he contemplated his next move. After consulting with his generals and advisors it was agreed that one serpent would not significantly increase their difficulties in recapturing the dragons and secondly as they were already on the outskirts of Den Dargo, they would hold their path and continue as planned. They did, however, divert their path and travelled on the North side of the forest and thus by avoiding Christiana he hoped to arrive in Ainslia faster. They had agreed that the few horsemen that had been frightened off previously would have been easy to scare, but an army such as this one must be able to get through whatever was between them and Ainslia. The Tranzicons were waiting. But worse than this the Hunti were on their way. Elgrade was in trouble.

THE TRANZICONS ATTACK ELGRADE'S ARMY

The Tranzicons were small, but they were fast and vicious. As soon as the army came in sight they attacked without warning. Disturbing the animals was their intent and they headed for the dogs first, diving headfirst into the beasts they drove their sharp head spikes in deep, withdrawing and attacking repeatedly. The distraught dogs started barking and jumping around, spinning to strike their attackers only to find themselves too late. They could not see their attacker and they became frightened and confused pulling on their chains and attacking each other. Jaques and the rest of the handlers tried desperately to control them but were unable to do so. Their fear was stronger than the leashes. Jaques encouraged his men to attempt to appear calm as the dogs sensed their panic and it made them even more determined to escape. There was a good deal of confusion and eventually the dogs were too strong and frightened to be contained, and they just ran off into the forest in panic. Their handlers followed them, partially to regain control of the dogs but they too were spooked and afraid. They were keen to escape as well. They were dog handlers, not fighters and although they were trying to recall the animals they were struggling to keep up. It would be a long time before they rejoined the fight, if indeed, they ever did. First, the terrified dogs would have to stop running long enough for the men, who were in pursuit, to catch up with them and then if they themselves had the heart to calm them enough to convince them to return to the battle-field. Jaques knew they would not return, with or without the dogs.

Although the men Cams' army were aware of the dogs becoming uncontrollable, they did nothing to try to contain them. It had nothing to do with them. This was the handler's business, and the men were often afraid of the dogs and would not go anywhere near them. Jakovyr, King Elgrade's Military Chief, was aware of the situation, but knew if the handlers were unable to settle them, he would not have any chance of containing them either. He decided to check out the War Beasts that were following the army behind the dogs.

Unfortunately for him the Tranzicon were now heading that way as well. Setting out with the same attack plan they had used on the dogs, they launched themselves onto the huge mammoth like ani-mals, but this time their spikes had negligible effect as the hair was too long and the skin too tough. Tomas gave an order to his army and the Tranzicons began to hum in unison, a queer high-pitched whine. Not everyone could hear it, but the Mammoths could, it hurt their ears and made their heads ache. They began to stamp and shake their massive heads. The ground trembled and everyone in the army felt that. The animals became panicked and pulled on their hobbles, their trainers trying to calm them with gentle words and giving them large flat biscuits they loved but none of this worked to soothe them in anyway at all. The handlers climbed up on the beast heads to settle them but all to no avail and the distressed animals began to stand up on their hind legs, anything to try to get relief from the pain in their ears.

Jakovyr came onto this scene, and he was horrified. Not seeing any reason for the disruptive behaviour of the herd he was at a loss what to do or how to help. 'It's a noise that's bothering them,' yelled Tanir, the chief handler, 'I've seen it happen before.' He was running around among the terrified beasts and shouting at the handlers, 'cover your beast's ears, use whatever you can find, stuff the ear canals and strap their ears down he yelled.' This took a while to get done but one by one the big animals began to quieten down. The Army had been held up and considerable damage had been caused by the out-of-control beasts. The Tranzicons were pleased with their efforts and began planning their attack on the horses, then later the men if necessary.

THE ARMIES CLASH

The dragons quickly reconnected with Thesso and Tarkin and told them they were going to pursue the Hunti even though they were aware that doing so would bring them into the path of Elgrade's army. They had sent a message via one of the swiftest elves, two days ago, telling King Paelion that Elgrade's Army was no longer planning to attack Christiana. He was marching directly to Ainslia. Josepheos hoped and trusted that by now the dwarfs were right behind Elgrade's army. Josepheos hoped they would catch up in time to provide himself, and the small army with him, a measure of protection. At the same time as sending this message directly to Paelion they once more contacted the dragons from Kriea. It was with great relief that they learned that there were dragons on their way to assist them in the battle.

Miriam, along with two of Tarkin's children, Karmen and Eske, remained with the villagers of Ainslia to protect them in case there was any direct attack. The village men and women, and the released servants from the dragon cavern had prepared themselves to fight. The village's children and elderly were on small boats heading out to sea. Miriam, with Karmen standing easily on her back, patrolled the skies above the village and above those fleeing to the safe island. Karmen's red hair flew out behind her catching the sun with an iridescent glow, providing a glimpse of her dragon heritage in the skies above Ainslia.

Meanwhile, King Paelion and his army had received the message from the dragons telling him King Elgrade's army had bypassed them and was heading straight for Ainslia. With this current information he quickly went from defence strategy to an offensive one and marched out after them.

This battle was not going to be an easy one, as they would have to fight the Hunti and then Cams Army must be stopped from injuring or capturing any of the dragons. King Elgrade did not know the Hunti were coming his way. He did not know what a Hunti was. So, the Dragons and Elves would have to fight the army and the Hunti until Elgrade realised he was under attack from more than one direction Paelion and the dragons were not his only problem. Even when he did realise, he was being attacked by something else, he would have no idea what it was, nor would he have any knowledge of how to defend himself.

It seemed that all the different parties would reach the Northern outskirts of the Enchanted Forest at the same time. Elgrade had marched that way to avoid an early encounter with Paelion. King Paelion had marched out to catch up with Elgrade. The Hunti could sense the army, which was very loud, and easily seen by the cloud of dust they were causing. The dragons, Josepheos and Shari, the elves and the half dragon, half human, descendants of Tarkin, were after the Hunti, moving directly into Elgrade's path.

Fathoms out to sea Thesso and Tarkin were moving through the water in haste, but it was still a long way to the trench, and they were becoming increasingly apprehensive of what was happening on shore.

Together they made the decision to leave the Chest in an underwater cave, in a reef that Thesso knew was close by. This was not the plan they had made but they felt the Chest would remain safe there. Firstly, if anyone found out where it was it would be exceedingly difficult for them to get to. If the worst happened, they would know immediately and would be able to intervene quickly. They knew the Chest would hold as the metal required to force it open was not available on Pardow. The Scarob Metal came from Igiasta and without the Portal Igiasta was not attainable. The Chest could not be damaged or forced open. Only Thesso and Tarkin using both their minds could open the Chest. They felt confident that all was safe, so they dove into the underwater cave and carefully hid the Chest inside, they could now return to land and join the battle. Even though Thesso could not spend too long on shore in the short periods of time that he could do so there was work he could do. As they swam back to shore, he sent a call out to all sea dragons to come to the area and to provide a protective guard for the cave. The remainder should come close to shore as he had previously asked them too.

Thesso also connected with the dragons of the other three great waters, Jodaw in the North, Francesca in the West and Jakeus in the South. He allowed them to see what was taking place here on the shores of the Eastern Ocean asking them to stand by to help if needed. He asked them to bring all their kin to assemble close to shore if they would be needed to come East and give protection to anyone, fleeing the fighting. They should also be ready to control the weather and tides as and when it would be helpful.

One party that had not made their way to the battle ground near the Enchanted Forrest was Mangara and his followers. They were not interested in doing any fighting and indeed were waiting impatiently until the battle had begun so that they could find and steal the Chest. Using wild birds as his ears he had messengers going all over the region and he was able to locate the groups of the Hunti by the energetic disturbance around them. He had followed them all the way to the village but was now waiting to observe the battle and to witness the dragon's fire, he also wanted a firsthand look at the dragon men and their ability to produce fire from their fingertips. Mangara was alarmed but also impressed by the thought of men fighting with fire. He simply could not comprehend this form of magic.

Staying in the shadows was what he did best, and when he saw the Chest being delivered via the large dragon Josepheos he could hardly stop himself from barging up the beach and demanding it be given to him. He, however, was not without caution, and he knew he did not have a chance of surviving such a risky and unplanned confrontation, his magic was no match for what was happening right in front of him. He would have to use stealth and up until now he had managed to remain undetected by the hypersensitive dragons. Watch and wait. When he witnessed, the Chest being taken to the beach by Tarkin he was filled with despair, and the sight of Thesso had him falling weeping to his knees. How would he find the Chest at sea, and if he did manage to locate it how would he attain it. After allowing himself a moment of despair he jumped to his feet and, to the astonishment of his followers, he quickly changed his shape to that of a giant sea eagle and flying high into the air he followed as the man climbed onto the huge sea serpent's head and the two dived into deeper water and headed out to sea.

'It's lost, it's lost,' the mantra played over and over in his head.

Then the Hunti attacked on the beach and the dragons retaliated with fire, he decided to return to shore before his feathers got scorched by bits of burning Hunti floating his way. He would not give up. He decided to do nothing, he would wait for the right opportunity to discover where the Chest was and find a way to get hold of it. He knew about the magical locks on the Chest, he did not know exactly what they were, but he would worry about getting it opened only when it was in his hands.

Word had spread of the movement of the troops, both men and dwarves, all the way to Metumia. Scouts had seen the dragons flying over to the East and South. One of their own was working in the city of Cam, looking after the huge beasts they used in battle. He had sent word home that they were preparing for a war. He could not advise them as to if and where they should stand. The moral ground was with the dragons and the dwarves that had risked their lives to rescue them. But the humans of Cam were human and not unlike them, only much smaller in stature. Did this matter? He had no information regarding the Chest, and he did not know that the Hunti were involved or indeed that they existed at all. He would wait to hear back from Yanji and Charlotte, the Metungian Elders who would decide where the Metungians would stand if and or when they had to join the war. Tanir would stand with his compatriots, whatever their choice. Meanwhile he looked after his charges, he was very fond of the huge animals.

THE HUNTI
ATTACK

Josepheos had been flying ahead of the group that was chasing the
fleeing Hunti when he heard the commotion ahead of him, he flew
directly up into the clouds, he wanted to get a better view of what was
causing the increase in noise and dust, but he wanted to avoid detec-
tion for as long as he could. The elves were running swiftly alongside
the battle grounds and indeed they were difficult to find, they had a
way of making themselves disappear. Lase led the big family group of
Tarkin's descendants, and they moved at a fast pace as well. Josepheos
was confused at first thinking that the Hunti were attacking the war
beasts but as he witnessed them having their heads wrapped up it did
not make too much sense. He was aware the Hunti were right on top
of the first warriors in Cam's army, but he had to get back to his own
group who were fast approaching the battle lines and King Elgrade
was oblivious as to what was about to fall upon him and his men.

Just as he turned to fly back to Shari and to tell his fighters
what was happening in front of them be heard the horses screaming,

they had sensed the Hunti and the Hunti had thrown them into a terrifying panic. Tomas, the tiny Tranzicon battle leader, felt the energy as well and called retreat with speed, he did not want his fellow Tranzicons to get caught between Elgrade's army and whatever this was. Elgrade's men were now sensing the energies as well and were looking, with panic in their eyes, towards the sky. The malicious energy of the Hunti was now becoming overwhelming and Jakovyr and his generals had to start giving out orders to the men. 'Hold your horses, get ready to fight.' Jakovyr screamed at the top of his lungs. 'Fight yes! But what?' was shouted back. Josepheos came roaring onto the scene, A fierce roar bellowed out of his mouth and fire erupted in front of him as he dived down onto the army below him, 'Dragon!' was screamed from every mouth. As they began to draw their bows and cross bows to fire, they saw the sky above them burst into balls of flame. They realised the dragon was fighting the energetic beings that were attacking them. Huge cheers arose from the army. They could now see what they were fighting and with the fire lighting up the Hunti they were able to direct their weapons accordingly.

Lase and his warriors along with the Elves where now running at an amazingly fast pace, and soon came upon the scene, Shari provided fire cover until they could get close enough to fight the Hunti, but they did not need it for long. Streams of fire leapt from the men's fingertips and the elves were right on target with their arrows. While Josepheos and Shari along with the others were fighting the Hunti, Elgrade gave the orders to his Generals to sound the order to retreat. He was in an unbelievably bad position, having two enemies to fight and not understanding who or what one of them was. He had also been attacked by something in Den Dargo, the war beasts were unsettled, and his dogs were gone, along with their trainers who were running behind them screaming unheard directions.

Retreat seemed his only option right now. He knew Elan's dwarf army was behind him but fighting them was preferable to what was in front of him. What he had just seen had shaken him to his core. Men streaming fire, elves fighting alongside humans, his own dragons with them, and he had been saved by this strange group, he was unable to comprehend what was happening in front of his own eyes, he needed information. They were fighting the weird energies because they had been attacked themselves, if so, what did it mean for him. Would he now be fighting, not only his dragons and a dwarf army but these supernatural humans, and elves? Were these elves from Cam? Did he not have an agreement with them? Elgrade needed to think about all of this and discuss with his advisors. He would also consult with Aurora his sorcerer, who was travelling with the army in case he needed her direction and information.

Back in the village Tarkin and Thesso returned to shore. They were aware of what was taking place on the outskirts of The Enchanted Forest but first they directed their attention on the village and its inhabitants. They discussed what to do with Eske, Carmen and Miriam and they all agreed that it was time to ensure the safety of all those unable to fight and complete the evacuation of Ainslia. Sea dragons had arrived onshore and were waiting to escort the fleets of small boats to the refuge island. Boats of children, the elderly and their carers had already left to go to the island but now everyone who was not involved in the villages defence was going to leave. This would keep them safe but also allow the fighters the freedom not to have to consider them during the battle. Also, they could not be taken hostage and used against them if they were out on the island. The sea dragons would provide protection going to the island and once there, they would not allow anyone to go ashore, even the villagers, without instructions from Thesso to do so.

The Hunti have fled their fire breathing attackers and had disappeared to the North. Thesso had no doubt that as soon as they were able to increase their numbers, they would begin their relentless quest for the Chest. Tarkin wanted to join the dragons and help in the battle that was inevitable now, as Elgrade had retreated directly into Paelion's forces. Thesso agreed with Tarkin and while Tarkin joined the fight he would stay here in the waters off Ainslia. He and Tarkin would as always hold mind contact. If necessary Thesso could control the weather and, he and Tarkin could exchange strength and power. With Miriam's permission Tarkin leapt onto her back, Carmen and Eske did the same. And jumped up alongside his. Now the fighters from the village were able to join the battle, they were no longer needed to defend the shores as the boats left. There was a feeling of anxiety and high energy around them but Thesso and the other sea dragons standing nearby gave them confidence.

THE BATTLE RAGES

When Elgrade retreated he had to turn his army around. The army usually marched with bowmen and crossbows and lance throwers in front, followed by soldiers on horseback. Then foot soldiers followed up the horses. The dogs with their handlers and the War Beast followed along behind. After these men came the backup groups. These groups consisted of servants that were cooks, cleaners, attendants, and dressers. There were Healers and Soothsayers, Magicians and Alchemists, Fortune Tellers, and Oracles. Horses and carts carried food and water. Animals such as pigs and cattle, for slaying, along with their shepherds followed these food carts. There were spare horses along with their grooms. There were also carts with medical supplies for the wounded and other carts for extra weapons. More foot soldiers followed. urning the army was a huge undertaking, and the reversal had to come about expediently as they were going to come up against Elan's army very soon. The dust and noise were seen and heard for miles. There was no question as to where the Army was at any given time. Elgrade ordered the crossbows to be behind the war beast this time as the dragons were behind them and only a crossbow or a lance, aimed with great skill could cause them any injury or possible kill them. The changing of the order of ranks added more confusion to the already hectic scene.

Clan Elan's army moved fast and was indeed fast approaching that of Elgrade. Unlike the human army the dwarves marched on foot. They did not have an entourage, no war beasts at all. They did not ride horses into battle. Each one carried his or her own food and water and weaponry. There were backup carts for extra weapons, these also served for whatever could not be carried personally. Dwarves are natural healers and it a commonly held skill amongst them. Paelion's Army was small in comparison to Elgrade's, but Paelion was aware that King Lombrok and his army was close by and would offer their assistance and boost his numbers. The three, freed dragons were on their way also and along with them Tarkin and his family of superhumans, or so he had heard. The two dwarf armies, the dragons, the superhumans and the elves, when combined would make a strong match for Elgrade's might.

Thornfoot and Hegal march at the front of the army, they were the first line of protection for the King who was up toward the front with his personal guard around him. Thornfoot looked back over his shoulder and scanned his kinsmen and women. Warriors all of them. He searched the ranks of dwarves for the team members he had just travelled to Cam with. They had bonded over the journey and their wellbeing concerned his thoughts. He wanted to meet their eyes to reassure them all. He caught Pria's eye first and a lump formed in his throat. She was so small in her breast plate and war attire, he wondered at her ability to carry her shield, but she appeared to do so without any effort. He knew her to be a fierce fighter. She was swift on her feet and always seemed to be two steps ahead of any combatant. He decided to watch her in the battle, Hegal too glanced over his shoulder and looked where Thornfoot was looking. He sighed and touched Thornfoot's shoulder. 'I'll be with you,' he said with the touch.

Thornfoot scanned for the others, Myrtle was close to Pria, Dwaymoon was right next to her, and Elkfast close as well, Thornfoot felt that they had decided to team up in the battle. He sought Treeturn and the others, they were in the same area, he nodded across to them and raised his hand. Turning back toward the front he silently asked the gods for their favour and leniency towards him and his kinsmen.

The two armies came into sight of each other just three miles inland from the coast, the edge of the massive volcano was on the south of Cam's troops and just beyond this the outskirts of the enchanted Forest. Clan Elans' Dwarf army was still partly in the Enchanted Forest where the trees and foliage were thicker.

Josepheos and Shari reached the rear of Cams army, they had stayed high above the clouds to safely get passed the rows of lancers and cross bows. It was unlikely that any of these could injure them as the skin of a dragon is ridiculously hard and well-guarded. Their scales were impenetrable, but there were few places where the scales were not so thick and here, they would be vulnerable. A dragon's eyes are mostly unprotected, his nostril openings, though small, would cause him or her considerable discomfort if penetrated with a spear. It was unlikely that this would bring the dragon down. There were other places as well. It would be a lucky shot that would get to any of these, but it was complacency that got you killed, so Josepheos took all precautions to protect himself and his family.

Josepheos was made aware that a fury of dragons was headed his way. Eleven had contacted him directly and informed him that they would arrive shortly and that more of his kin had heeded his call for help and were flying to join the battle. He had hoped the arrival of the first eleven would have happened before the armies met but that was not going to be achieved, they were a still few hours away and may not arrive together due to them coming from all points on the compass. Dragons were assembling from all over Pardow. If they had arrived all together the sight may have caused Elgrade to decide to withdraw and run all the way back to Cam. The unfortunate truth was that the battle was now inevitable.

As the two armies, Elgrade's and Paelion's, were marching toward confrontation, the elves were closing in along the edges of Cam's army, having covered the distance between them at a great speed allowing them to out flank the soldiers. Paelion had the battle horn sounded, the noise was both exhilarating and terrifying, no one could miss it. His bowmen proceeded to shoot at the oncoming army. He had not hesitated, he did not address his troops, he knew they understood the art of war as solidly as he did. They would do their job. Hearing the command of the horn the elves appeared from the tree line, as if by magic, and they too fired their arrows. They would fire and then immediately disappear back into the shadows of the forest's foliage. They became an invisible and therefore impossible, target.

Elgrade's bowmen retaliated, the lancers and crossbow operators scanned the skies for the dragons. They did not have long to wait as Josepheos and Shari burst from the clouds and dived onto their position. They were seared with fire, their eyes momentarily blinded by the smoke, and their weapons made useless by the smog and fire in the air. The two dragons worked together to forge a line of flames between the opposing armies. They rose to the sky as swiftly as they had appeared, now and again taking time to pluck a couple of the cross bows and their operators, the men with their feet still in the stirrups hardly had time to realise the peril they were in before it was all over for them. They dragons would carry the terrified men, kicking and screaming, up into the sky before dropping them back into the midst of the army. The crossbow operators and the lancers were now so scared of the dragons that they neglected their own positions, and the air became safer for Josepheos and Shari.

The armies continued to engage, and Clan Elan's bow men kept firing through the smoke and haze. Dust rose from the ground and there was noise and yelling, and cries of pain filled the air. While a host of arrows were meeting their mark others were falling on to raised shields thus forcing the men and women to protect themselves and making them ineffective in the fight.

The men and dwarves were fighting hand to hand as well as they were now in close contact. The bows and arrows were no longer the preferred weapon and swords and hammers were brought into the fight. Elgrade's army pushed their horse men to the front. Their added height and bulk gave the riders an advantage over the smaller dwarfs of the ground. Josepheos and Shari, seeing this turned their attention to the horses, frightening them and causing them to unsaddle their riders. The elves running alongside the army also turned their attention to the horses, bringing them down with well-aimed arrows. The fighting continued, there were one-to-one fights all over the battlefield, but it was the dragons who were making the difference for the Dwarf King's army.

To even things up for his men, who were taking the worst of it from the dragons and dwarves, Elgrade ordered his War Beasts to be brought through to the front of the fighting. His army parted and the huge beasts were pushed through. Their mammoth bodies crushed whatever was in their paths. Thornfoot slowed his pace forward, as much to avoid the beasts as to get closer to his old team members. The dragons now swooped in on the war beasts, Tarkin astride Miriam had joined forces with Josepheos and Shari. An extra dragon was a bonus, and Tarkin from his vantage point on Miriam's head was feeding the battle pictures back to Thesso. Eske and Carmen had been set down into the battle and were now fighting their way through to the

War Beasts. Fire was flying from their fingers as arrows whirled past them.

Tarkin pushed down asking Miriam to take him on top of the beasts and the two older dragons followed them down. They could not slow the charge of the beasts as the sight and smell of the dragons was terrifying them and added to this their handlers were driving them into the battle ahead of them. Tarkin and Miriam swooped in and plucked a trainer from the leading War Beast and Josepheos and Shari did the same. Tanir saw all of this, so he ducked his head and holding onto the side of his mount he slipped from the War Beast's back. This was not an easy task at full gallop, and he was also hindered by the warriors on the ground. Careful to avoid being trampled to his death he worked his way behind the line of beasts. The animals were now stampeding out of control.

'Turn them!' Tarkin screamed aloud but also via mind connection to his children and to the other dragons. The Superhumans ran at incredible speed directly at the beasts, with Elvin skills they ran up the sides of the beasts, grabbed the fallen reigns and they pulled the heads of the beast s till they had no choice but to turn their bodies to match this alignment. The beasts were now being pushed back into Cam's ranks. Nearby elves jumped unto the backs of the beasts and while the beasts were being turned by the Superhumans, the elves were standing upright, in perfect harmony with the twisting, turning animals, and all the time they were firing their arrows into Cam's men. There was so much confusion in Cam's ranks as suddenly, they were now the ones in danger of being trampled by their own War Beasts. They were also facing an onslaught of arrows being fired from these War Beasts backs.

Jakovyr saw the situation, which was not a good one for his men, as their battle formation was to spear head the middle of the attack. The men were now reclosing the gap they made for the beasts to come through and were pushing forward to regain the formation. He decided to call a retreat. Bugles shouted out the urgent message and the men began to respond. Elgrade's guard was the first to respond and they quickly surrounded the King and began to manoeuvre his horse to the edge and Northern side of the battle. Keeping the volcano on their Southern and Eastern side they retreated to the North. The army followed slowly, hampered by their own entourage, which was now in front of them, they were taking heavy casualties.

Tanir tried to regroup the beasts' handlers to get them back under control, even to calm them a little. He understood what Tarkin was doing, and he knew that, tactically, the move was brilliant and unexpected. Unexpected because the Superhuman strength of Tarkin's kin was what made it possible. No other beings would have been able to control the beasts' direction so easily and so speedily. To Tanir's dismay his trainers had no heart to attempt any sort of control of the animals and had already joined the troops fleeing to the North. He thought to try, by himself, to turn the lead beast and direct them into the forest but the shooting arrows of the elves made getting close to the beasts difficult. He felt if he could head them to the trees, they would take the opportunity to go for cover themselves. Tanir knew this was not going to be the answer when he saw elves racing along the tree line firing into the mammoths, they could not bring them down, but they could keep them moving. Tanir made a sad but necessary decision, and he turned his face to the North and ran with the Army.

During all this fighting and turmoil Tarkin noticed that Miriam was struggling to keep herself in the air. She had been diving on the beasts and had taken a stray arrow that had hit her in one of her huge wings. It had not brought her down but as the tear got bigger it was hampering her balance in the air. She would have to land. Tarkin scanned for the right place and Miriam was doing the same, there was a lot going on below her and she was unable to see a large enough space where she would not be in more danger, Tarkin called in Josepheos and Shari and they arrived in the sky above Miriam within seconds. They used their huge bodies and fire breathing to force the beasts wide, they landed themselves, providing a safe area for her to alight down also. A little clumsily she met the ground between her Mum and Dad, she did not suffer further injuries in the landing.

As if appearing out of nowhere Cara the Elf Councillor joined the group around Miriam, she nimbly climbed up Miriams side and gently examined her outstretched wing. The tear was large and would need repairs. A dragon has self-healing powers, but it would take too long to fill the hole in the wing membrane. Time was something they did not have in the current situation. Everyone was talking and trying to think at the same time. Cloth would have to be used to patch the hole was the final decision and Thornfoot who had joined the dragons to see what he could do, started to run back to the supply carts to see if he could find anything that could be used. Caro said she would be able to sew the cloth and attach it to the wings.

This solution presented as the only option that could work in the situation they were in, when suddenly there was an unusual buzz in the air around them, and in particular, around Miriam's wing. A hundred small birdlike creatures had arrived and were flying in all directions across the wounded wing. In amazement everyone realised they were weaving an exceptionally fine vine across the hole. The Tranzicons from Den Dargo were doing what they did best, they were weaving. It did not take too long and the tear in Miriam's wing was completely covered with the web of vine, and Tomas, one of the leaders of the Tranzicons asked her to try her wing and see if she good fly. After she had flexed and raised her wing she extended it fully, she declared that it was good, and she would be able to fly. As she rose slowly into the air assessing her wing as she gained height the Tranzicons flew around her for a while longer to make sure she was fine, when they had reassured themselves, she was flying perfectly, they left as quickly as they arrived.

Thornfoot was running hard back to the supply carts in search of suitable cloth for Miriam's wing when he saw Pria in a particularly lop-sided contest with a human twice her size. Dwaymoon was not in his usual position, by her side. She was moving fast and delivering blows where she could, but it was obvious to Thornfoot she could not dodge or outrun her opponent for much longer. Without hesitation, giving no thought for himself, he darted across the front of the stampeding War Beasts to reach her. He had almost crossed the line of panicked animals when one of the large beasts fell, exhaustion, or too many arrows, had finally brought it down. Two of the elves, which were riding on it to gain the height advantage to use their bows, leapt from its back and tried to grab Thornfoot out of its path, but they were unable to get to him quickly enough. He went down under the huge animal. As he lay there, he looked across at Pria, she was screaming at him to, 'get up.' As the two elves took on her assailant she started to run towards him. Thornfoot did not feel any pain, he saw her coming and smiled at her, then amazingly, as he knew his wife was with the children and elderly back in Christiana, he saw her running behind Pria, Therese reached out her arms and throwing herself down on the ground beside him, she embraced him. He tried to tell her everything was going to be fine as he reached out to return her embrace. He was no longer able to see Pria as his eyes would not focus. Silently, in the loving embrace of his darling Therese, Thornfoot left the battle.

Meanwhile messengers had been running all over informing where and what was happening in each of the other armies. Josepheos informed Paelion that Lombrok had turned his army to the North, after receiving information that Cam had retreated that way. Lombrok decided he and his army would travel North of the Enchanted Forest, if he could move fast enough, he would be able to cut off the retreating Cam army.

At this point in the battle Elgrade was not planning a retreat or a surrender, but he needed to regroup and needed to get his team of War Beasts under control, which was if any had survived the turmoil. He was disappointed when Tanir had sent information that he was unable to recall the handlers and that as far as he could say the beasts were too afraid of the dragons to be of any help. The plan to bring down the dragons and give the beasts a better chance at doing injury to them, had not worked. The dragons were simply too big, too quick, and too smart. Tanir's advise to the war chiefs was that they should round up the War Beasts and they should be returned to Cam. King Elgrade stomped and stewed when he heard this, he knew that Tanir was right, and his army did depend on the War Beasts to break up enemy lines and destroy their formations, it would be foolhardy to keep them here and potentially lose them when they were having little effect on this battle, in fact they were doing as much harm as good. First the dogs and now them, he was losing his confidence along with his war machine. Reluctantly he agreed with Tanir and sent him off on this task. Tanir set out trying to firstly find his handlers and he hoped that they would then go with him in search of the panicked beasts. Tanir had already decided he would not return to Cam but would make his way, with the beasts, home, to Metumia.

Elgrade's scouts had returned, and they had brought with them more unwelcome news. Dragons had been seen flying towards their location and Lombrok's army was marching to the North to holt their retreat. He sat with his counsel and advisors. There was Lombrok to the North, a small army but one with an enormously powerful reputation for destroying larger ones. They could not be taken lightly. Then there was Paelion's army of Dwarves, Dragons, Elves and Superhumans and Humans to the West. There were more dragons flying to the battlefield to support those already fighting. His own dragons, the legendary Dragons of Cam, that he had dealt with dishonourable for years, were leading the battle against him. His father had made an agreement of mutual protection and support with the two older dragons which he had not only broken but he had imprisoned them. For over a hundred years they had been locked up. He, himself, had upheld his father's decision to imprison them. He could lay no blame at his fathers' feet. He had the power, and he should have altered the way the dragons were treated in Cam. His dogs had gone mad in Den Dargo. What had caused this was unknown, but whatever it was it had sided with the Dragons. Hundreds of his troops were dead and more injured. A sizeable number of these deaths were caused by his own War Beasts. Then right at the start there were those strange energetic creatures that the dragons and superhumans had fought off. Where had they come from? What were they? Why had the dragons and elves helped his army by attacking them? There were too many questions to answer, and with very few positives to support their continued fighting, the outcome of all this discussion was that the most honourable decision would be to attempt to negotiate a peaceful resolution to the situation. Elgrade wanted to consult Aurora for her predictions and then he would make his decision. Unless she had something amazing to tell him he would have to try to negotiate his way out of the mess he was in.

Elgrade's mood was extremely low as he returned to his tent. Hundreds of good, and loyal men had been lost to his arrogance and impetuousness. Aurora had already been sent for so he sat with his head in his hands waiting for her to arrive. He never heard her come into the room so when she quietly addressed her King he jumped into the air. This made him laugh and after that he felt a little better, even if a little less Kingly. She had already set up her accruements and began gazing into the oily waters. 'There are at least seventeen dragons arriving within hours. That is the dragons I can see, but there are more waiting for the call to come. You will not be able to fight them. There is a mist arising from the east that may provide opportunity for a retreat, but it may leave you more vulnerable when it lifts. If you negotiate you must do so with humility and with honour, then you will have a good outcome for your people. You will lose somethings in negotiations.' She looked up at him and continued, 'I see you smiling as you ride home to Cam, why I cannot see. But you will survive the negotiations at least.' Aurora lifted her head and spoke directly to Elgrade, 'There is no straightforward way here, you must look inside yourself, see who you are, and act without fear. May the gods favour you tomorrow.' Packing up her bowl and oils, she left the room.

Elgrade sat in deep contemplation. The mist may help them to withdraw but they were not a quiet group. They would have to know exactly where Lombrok was holding his army, if he moved, they would not see it. If they walked directly into his army then they would be forced to fight in close combat. Too many had already died, and what for, his pride? He knew that no matter what he decided to do the dragons would not be returning to Cam. Tomorrow morning, he would send an emissary to King Paelion.

Jakovyr chose two of his men. Not his generals but not low-ranking men either. They would raise a white flag and ride out at dawn, into Clan Elan's camp. He, and the remaining generals would ride behind, be visible, but not so close to be killed if Paelion chose not to negotiate.

The delegation would ask for a conference between King Paelion, Josepheos and King Elgrade, or their delegates. He did not mention King Lombrok in the request as at this point, he was not supposed to be aware of his presence. If he appeared willing to negotiate now, while he still had an option to retreat, if may go better for him, best to keep quiet about the fact he was aware of Lombrok's army to the north of their position.

At first light the next day, Jakovyr's chosen men rode out in front of a small column of men, Jakovyr rode with the column, but he would not go forward until an official agreement had been made. This was an extremely dangerous time for them all as they would be at the mercy of their enemies. A safe return was never guaranteed in these situation and a times an emissary would be returned to his own lines with his head on a pole, a very descriptive and final expression that there would be no negotiations. Everyone was dressed in high regalia, to show their own importance as much as to show respect to the importance they put on the mission today. The two men riding at the front raised a white flag as they saw the dwarf camp ahead of them. The riders behind halted to await their return, alive or dead.

As they approached the dwarves' first line of sentries they were challenged. King Elgrade's man stated their request, and they were soon surrounded by Clan Elan's warriors. They were hastily taken back to the area where the councillors were talking with the dragons. Two of the councillors walked out to meet them.

After the formalities of greeting each other one of the messengers addressed the group, a rehearsed message. 'We have come directly from King Elgrade, he wishes to meet to discuss a negotiated end to this conflict. He asks a meeting between himself and King Paelion and Josepheos,' the elder of the dragons. The councillors listened, nodded, laughed, and went back to the others. The Councillors returned promptly, 'we will discuss with him his terms of surrender, nothing else.' 'We will meet here at noon, King Elgrade and his councillors will come unarmed, King Paelion and his councillors will meet with him. The dragons will attend remotely, and that is that. You have till noon to accept or be prepared to resume the fight.'

Jakovyr was excited to see his men returning with their heads intact. But on receiving the message from Paelion, Elgrade, on the other hand, was furious. He had been rejected, his desire to negotiate totally dismissed. Surrender or fight! Truthfully, Elgrade was aware of his position, and Paelion was no fool. He would have to pay for his folly, but at least he had a meeting to plead his case. He knew he did not have any legitimate case. He had marched out of the gates of Cam in a fury. He had not even waited for his own delegates to return from Christiana, if he had he would have discovered that King Paelion had no knowledge of the dragons' escape. He would have to throw himself on the mercy of the leaders of the parties involved. He was not exactly sure who was involved but he was positive that he was on his own. He thought on this and realised the dragons he had held captive had made him complacent, he did not need any back up with them in his artillery. So, he had no one to call on when this part of his artillery was turned against him. He called his advisor and council, and they began to discuss what they may realistically request and what they could offer in return. Elgrade hung on to the words of his fortune teller, that he would return alive to Cam. He had to try to get these same results for his men.

Elgrade rode into Christiana's camp at precisely noon. He was escorted to a large table in the centre of a clearing. There were seven beings already seated at the table. King Paelion, his Chief Advisor Graynor and Moon Ray and Hegel as Military Advisors. Two elves, Caro and Eidsvold, were present and one human, well partially human, Tarkin. They all sat patiently awaiting his arrival. The dragons were nowhere to be seen. There were seats for just two more. King Elgrade dismounted with help from his men and walked to the table, he bowed his head to King Paelion and turned and invited his own Chief Military adviser, Jakovyr, to join him. He was offered the seat directly across from Paelion and Jakovyr sat by his side. On the other side of Elgrade sat Graynor. Hegal sat beside Jakovyr. No sudden moves were expected but were adequately prepared for. The dragons were indeed close by and were in mind contact with Tarkin all the time. Thesso too was listening in.

A list of what Christiana would consider acceptable was presented to Elgrade. A young dwarf, standing behind the table, facing Elgrade, presented the list in a loud clear voice.

'Recompense must be paid for the deaths caused. The number of Widows would increase, and children would be left without a mother or father as often, both parents were lost to the battle. The city would have to care for them and Elgrade must contribute to this.'

'Safe passage for the Elves to return to their homes and the area of Cam where they live to continue to be theirs with no penalty. A compensation for their losses as well. A treaty of no harm toward them be put in place, and they are to be allowed free trade with Cam as before the war.'

'Never again was Elgrade or his successors to be allowed hold a dragon against their will. To never attack any dragon anywhere and to provide haven to all dragons if they requested it.'

'He was required to provide a hostage for three years to assure all of this was put in place. This hostage was to be of high ranking. He, or she would be given the concession of bringing their immediate family with them. They would come to no harm unless the agreement was breached.'

Elgrade looked at Jakovyr, it was what they had expected, better actually, no lives had been asked, he was immensely relieved that he had not lost any more men. He agreed to all terms and would negotiate on compensation. It was fortunate that he had agreed because during the night the extra dragons had arrived at the battle site. They were tucked nicely into the background with Josepheos, Miriam, who was healing very well, and Shari. Finally, the compensation was agreed on and Jakovyr had stepped forward as a hostage if they were satisfied as to his rank and character. The dwarves were satisfied, and they accepted him as their hostage, he would stay with them now, and his family would be escorted to him at the proper time. Jakovyr could not say exactly how he felt about this, but in someways he felt relief, better to be in Christiana with the dwarves, living a peaceful life than in Cam listening to a depressed and disgruntled Elgrade ranting and raving for months on end. Overall, he decided he could do little other than accept the next three years, so there was little point in worrying.

While all of this was taking place the Hunti have made their way back to the fighting, taking energy from all the pain and suffering. They had been growing stronger feeding on the fear and confusion the dragons and the huge beast stampeding was causing. It all added to the mayhem and panic. The Hunti loved it. They did not need to do anything themselves just feed on the suffering before them. Hunti have no allegiance they only care for themselves, not even the plight of their fellow beings evokes any kind of kinship or sympathy, they hunt in packs because there is more success that way, if they find nothing to feed on, they will very quickly and aggressively turn their energy toward each other. The men and the beasts had sensed them again, but the men were under attack. They could not see the Hunti, but they could see their enemy approaching with raised weapons and an intent to kill, they fought what they could see. The dragons had been breathing fire and singeing multitudes of Hunti and after a short while, their numbers dwindled once more, and they began to drift away from the battle. As they left the armies, they returned to Mangara on the beach in Ainslia in the hope he had located the Chest.

MANGARA GOES
AFTER THE CHEST

Mangara presented a disturbing sight. His hair stood on ends and here and there it was burnt off completely, his clothes, which had always been eccentric, were in tatters, ribbons of cloth flying in all directions tossed and twirled by the sea breeze. His beard was also singed, and his face was blackened with soot. His eyes, wide and delusional, stared widely out of his gaunt face, darting this way and that at a rapid rate. His followers had all but left him. The more sensible one had joined the Ainslia villagers and had been ferried to the safe island for protection from the battle, others stayed loyal to him, as much out of having no other viable choice, than a belief in him and his rantings. Curiosity as to what he would produce next was also of interest to them, he was, if nothing else, entertaining. Despite all these setbacks Mangara was not defeated, he may have looked that way, but he was not. He had a plan.

Mangara remembered a significant detail from earlier when he was attempting to follow Thesso and Tarkin out to sea, he had noticed that they had returned, not long after he had started to get burnt from the falling debris, quite a bit sooner than he had predicted. They did not have the Chest with them so they must have left it somewhere not too far offshore, underwater he assumed. He called his faithful few and told them they would go after the Chest as soon as darkness was upon them. He needed a boat, and he asked them to find one. They were not to touch it till after dark. Despite that the villagers were now out to sea he still felt that there were too many eyes and ears to witness their movements in the daylight. Mangara needed to use the boat to get as far offshore as he could before he would shape change again, and not into a bird this time.

Later that night before the orbiting sun lit the sky, he put his plan into action. His followers had secured a small rowboat, and they were now rowing silently out to sea. Mangara was directing their path. There was lots of movement in and under the water, huge beasts circled lazily here and there but as he got out deeper, he noticed their number had increased and more of them were patrolling a particular area. 'This is the place,' he whispered excitedly. 'I must be in the water to take on my new shape this time, please try to recover my clothing for me. The men exchanged amused glances, but no one was brave enough to laugh. 'Of course,' They replied.

Mangara sank into the water over the side of the boat, his clothing popped up and they carefully retrieved it with one of the oars. They could laugh now, and they did, but they stopped abruptly when a large squid rose up out of the water beside the boat and gave them all a good squirt of black ink. Mangara sank back into the water pleased with his own ingenuity. A squid, with eight arms, he could easily carry the Chest back to the boat with these arms. He allowed himself one lovely, fleeting feeling of pleasure. In this state of self-satisfaction Mangara did not take the time to think about anything unconnected to his quest.

This was a mistake because hiding in the dark was something horrible.

The eel is an apex predator. He hunts at night. He is smooth and almost motionless as he moves silently through the water, he has razor sharp teeth. Extremely territorial and with a keen sense of smell he is always on the alert. Tonight, the extra activity and the frequent visitors to and from the underwater cave had him sensitive to even the smallest movement. He realised he could smell something that he partially recognised but there is something not right about it. This had been an unusual day with all the huge sea dragons moving around disturbing the seabed and eating what should have been his dinner. It was okay though as they disturbed smaller prey, and he could catch it as it fled in panic away from them. Earlier today a large dragon came directly into his cave at the bottom of the reef. The huge serpent did not stay long but he left something behind, and this inedible thing was now in his territory. Suddenly he recognised the distinct smell of octopus, one of his favourite foods. There was still an unfamiliar smell hanging around, so it was with extreme caution he poked his great head with its two rows of razor-sharp teeth out into the cave to observe the scene. Near the Chest he saw the octopus, nothing else. It was a large one and he was hungry. He did not hesitate to strike. One large bite from his incredibly flexible jaws and he had him. The octopus fought feebly for a while, but it was not a fair fight, before he even recognised what had hit him, he was already halfway down the eel's digestive tract.

ELGRADE MAKES
A RETREAT

On leaving the negotiating table King Elgrade was not too sure how to feel. He was still alive. That was a good start. It was not guaranteed earlier this morning and despite Aurora's prediction of him returning to Cam he had been concerned his own life may be required. He was not a coward, but he knew his son was too young to take his place, chaos would be Cam's reward for his folly if his life had been demanded. But they had not killed him, and indeed the Dwarf King had dealt with him with more generosity and mercy that he would have given had the roles been reversed. He would withdraw his army and return to Cam. He would return with nothing gained and less then he had come with.

Already Elgrade's advisors had been organising the army to mobilize and to return to Cam. Jakovyr would not be accompanying them home. The men loved and respected him, and their heads were down along with their morale. Better if we had left the King instead, they thought, but none mentioned it aloud. Elgrade rode in the middle of the retreating forces, as he usually did, he felt defeated and angry. He was angry with himself. Everything that had gone wrong was his fault and despite his advisors pointing out that the result of the negotiating was not as bad as it could have been, he felt the weight of his impetuous nature.

Elgrade's advisors pointed out that apart for the loss of treasure and Jakovyr's incarceration everything else worked as well for them as for the groups involved. They needed the Elves to stay as they supplied a good percentage of Cam's fresh food. They were also exceptionally good and generous healers, often not asking reward for this. The Kingdom would not have control over them, but did it ever have control. Elgrade listened as he rode. He looked up at the sky to see the dragons had decided to accompany them to Cam. Flying overhead they stayed high so as not to alarm the animals.

He could not help thinking of his dragons and why he had kept them captured. They had been loyal and had never shown any signs of aggressive toward him or his citizens. They had given him a mode of protection nothing else had. His realm was at peace because of them. Now that was lost. He felt increasingly sorry for himself as he gazed at their splendour. So many colours, shapes, and sizes were on display. Wings flashed in the sun and glistened with rays of light. Incredibly beautiful, he thought. It was at this moment he had a brilliant idea.

Cam had lost three dragons, and he was returning with thirty dragons. Was that not a boon? Was that not a triumph? He excitedly called his advisors to him. 'Send a fast messenger to Cam, prepare a space for all the dragons to rest and prepare a grand celebration with music, food, and festivities. I will present the dragons with the terms of the treaty that we have already negotiated. It will be a great ceremony.'

For the first time in days Elgrade felt positive, this was a good outcome for him and the dragons. they would have freedom of movement and safe refuge, and he would be a hero, Cam would be assured of dragons forever. With time, constant care, and attention he felt sure he could persuade one of them to supply his anti-aging needs.

THESSO PREPARES
A TRAP FOR
THE HUNTI

The Hunti were on their own, they no longer had Mangara to help them to attain the Chest. Mangara was gone, and all his followers had dispersed. The Hunti were always solely focused on obtaining the Chest and had no concern at all for Mangara or his fate. Once more they were concentrating their efforts on finding the Chest's whereabouts. They knew that Thesso and Tarkin held the key to its location, so they turned their energies towards Ainslia where they had last seen the pair. Of course, this led them to Thesso who was always very aware of their presence and was expecting their appearance. Thesso felt that this was a fantastic opportunity to get rid of them, their numbers were down, and they were all hanging around the area, seeking any opportunity for information. Could he find a way to trap them all. He began to formulate a plan that he had been mulling over in the back of his mind for months now.

Thesso connected to his counterparts of the seas in the North, South and West. Working together they could form a weather pattern that the Hunti could not escape. Wind and rain were needed. A little electrifying lightening would help too. Thesso would create a strong wind that would force the Hunti North, directly into a storm that Jodaw, the Sea Dragon that controlled the Northern Oceans, had been preparing for this moment. He had been holding warmer air in the atmosphere above the North Sea, holding it in a swirling pattern, waiting for the call from Thesso. Now he had that summons he began to pull the warmer air down into the cooler air beneath. As it fell it expanded into the air around it and as it grew it pulled more warm air down, thus creating a monster storm which now only had to be directed toward the fleeing Hunti.

Thesso called on the winds that blew over the Eastern seas, asking them to blow inland and to the North. The wind obeyed and powerful wind gusts blew into the Hunti and forced them North where Jodaw was waiting with a perfect storm. The Hunti were being buffeted and bashed by the fierce winds, and legions were lost. A quick-thinking group of them managed to move faster and using their fellow Hunti to shelter from the worst of the wind were able to continue North. They happily soaked up the energy of those falling apart around them and thus were able to survive. As they moved out of the wind they moved directly into the path of an electrical storm of tremendous power. Hundreds were struck by lightning, and others were forced to the ground by the weight of the water. Hunti could not survive in water, so these died where they fell. The remaining Hunti trying to flee West or South were met with similar fates. To the South Jakeus had been busy creating a layer of warm air that blew high over the south sea, and now he allowed the cool air on the ocean meet this warm moist wind. This contact caused the warm air to cool rapidly which created a fog of formidable dimensions. This dense fog rose upward and blinded any being flying over the South Sea. The sheer weight and density of the fog made it difficult for the Hunti to navigate through and soaked and blinded they fell to the ground in vast numbers and dissipated into the air around them. To the West Franchesca was playing her part by creating Mini tornados that were spinning anywhere they wanted, swirling and destroying any Hunti that hoped to escape in this direction. This terrible weather lasted days to make sure not one Hunti escaped or survived. As these fierce weather patterns were occurring only where the Hunti flew, Elgrade's celebrations were not affected nor was the return home of the triumphant dwarf armies.

KING PAELION RETURNS TO CHRISTIANA

King Paelion led his warriors back to Christiana and home. They had been victorious and had achieved what they want to, but a price had been paid. Lives were lost, and faces were solemn, but heads were held high as they moved along. Pria walked slowly, she held her head high also despite the pain she felt, not just physical but the pain of loss, her dear friend and their fearless team leader had fallen in the battle others from their team had died or were injured but she maintained her strength and pride, she wanted them to be proud of her. They had made the amazing journey to find the dragons, but they had not all made it through the battle. Dwaymoon was injured and rode home in a wagon. He would heal but the scars would be there forever. Pria had visited him as the hospital wagons were moving out and he had pledged his love for her, she told him she felt the same way and reciprocated his love. They held each other and wept. So much had been lost but honour remained.

On their march home King Paelion asked Myrtle to arrange a meeting with the Tranzicons so that they might be officially thanked for their help in the fight. King Paelion rode out with all his splendour and a great and impressive entourage accompanied to meet the Tranzicon. The Tranzicons had flown out of their beautifully woven nests to meet the King. There was a huge amount of buzzing and fluttering going on. Mrytle happily translated much of this banter for King Paelion. He formally thanked them for their heroism, especially against such massive odds, and he then made a solemn declaration that Den Dargo was to be their sanctuary, and they would now have control over all the Enchanted Forest.

Tarkin had returned to the beach and was walking with Thesso. Thesso shared the fate of the Hunti with him in detail and Tarkin was relieved to see them gone for good. Tarkin had been able to see glimpses here and there as to what was happening with the Hunti, but he was distracted with the events happening in the aftermath of the battle. Thesso was given the full run down on Elgrade's retreat and the negotiated surrender he had made. Overall, it was not a terrible outcome. Among the deaths the loss of Thornfoot was particularly hard for them accept, the courageous act of protecting Pria had cost him his life, but they all agreed it was just like him to sacrifice himself for his brothers and sisters of the clan. Josepheos, Shari and Miriam joined them via mind contact and they grieved together. The dragons had not known Thornfoot for long, but he had proved himself over and over to be worthy of their love and praise. His courage in battle and his ingenuity when he led the rescue mission to free the dragons of Cam had impressed them all. He had been a friend to all dragons, and he was gone. Stories would be told for generations about his courage, intelligence, his bravery, and his ingenuity, tears would fall in his memory and many a hearty laugh and a full tankard of ale, would be shared over the story of his first dragon ride.

TANIR GOES TO METUMIA

After days of searching through the countryside Tanir had only been able to locate and round up three of the war beasts. The other handlers had left and gone home, so he was alone as he led the beasts along the pathways in the lower mountain regions. He had decided straightaway not to take the beasts back to Cam. He would take them up into the mountain ranges on his way home and he would free them. He was determined to let them live in peace, they had been treated badly and been used as weapons of war for long enough. It was time they were free. When he reached the valleys in the foothills leading up into the Metumia ranges he let them free, he removed all their war apparel and armour and the chains and hobbles on their legs. He led them to a creek in one of the deepest valleys and left them there. He silently hoped the other beasts that he had not been able to find and had been forced to leave behind, would be able to track these three and be reunited with them. Tanir wondered where Jaques was with the war dogs, had he found them. He sighed, not much made sense today. Finally, having searched everywhere he could think of to find the remainer of the beasts, including climbing the highest hill around, he decided he had done all he could, he began the climb up into the mountain crater that was his home.

The Metungians met him with excitement and joy, he had been gone a long time. They were eager to get news of what was happening to the South and East of them. They had seen the dragons flying over their land and had witnessed the weather, which had been crazy in all directions. After receiving food and drink Tanir sat down with his Elders and began to recall all that had happened to him, to the war beasts, to the humans of Cam. He described the battle and the fighting that had gone on. He spoke sadly of the deaths and injuries, how the dogs had been panicked by something they could not see, and that the army itself they had been attacked by something very alarming. A spirit or many spirits, was the only way he could describe what had taken place, and it was only when the dragons arrived, intervening on their behalf, despite them being at war with the same dragons, that these weird spirit beings had been chased off or destroyed. Another remarkable factor in this battle was the numbers of species that were fighting as teams. Fighting alongside the dragons were a group of humans, led by a man called Tarkin, they had unbelievable powers, of strength and speed. They also had the ability to produce fire from their fingertips. Elves fought alongside the Dragons, Dwarfs and Humans, something he had never experienced. A more confusing war could not be imagined and there were so many things he had never in his long life encountered nor could explain.

Tanir was able to tell them that victory was to the Dwarves and Dragons and thus his Human army was in retreat. After listening to his story, he was sent off to rest and recuperate from his long trek while the elders sat down to talk all this information through. They thought that the biggest question was what the fighting was about.

After debating the prudence of getting involved or of staying safely hidden away, they decided that it would be in their best interest to know what was happening outside their crater home. Too much was changing, and they should know what and how any of it affected them and their families. Yanji and Charlotte and Tanir along with a small group from the village, would go to Ainslea and talk with the man Tarkin.

Tarkin and Thesso were laying in the shallows, they were alone because the men and women of Ainslia had not returned to the village. After the battle and Elgrade's surrender and retreat the fighters had joined the rest of the village on the island refuge and they had all decided to simply stay to relax and recover from the excitement and fear of war. Taking a rest themselves, Tarkin and Thesso were discussing how the Portal should be dealt with now the Hunti offered no threat. The Portal had caused two wars already and considerable pain and destruction to those who had answered the call to protect it, so perhaps it ought to be permanently destroyed, but such a loss was unthinkable to Thesso. Hiding it deep in an active volcano had seemed to be perfect solution, or so they had thought, but the Portal had resurfaced with the dying of the volcano and the mining of the dwarves. Would the deep-sea trench be enough. How could, they be sure.

The only place the Chest could be opened, without Tarkin and Thesso joining their minds, was Igiasta. In Igiasta you would find the Scarab metal that was needed for the destruction of the Chest. All of this was in theory as you would require the use of the Portal to get to Igiasta to obtain the metal. It was unlikely that anyone could achieve this impossible task. Tarkin suggested they use the Portal and leave it on any planet or world other than Igiasta, of course, so that if it were found, it could not be opened without him and Thesso. This sounded good in theory but to use the Portal the Disc which contained the

Portal would have to be being held by Tarkin or Thesso, so how would they return to Pardow without it. Ideas, both good and bad, were considered and dismissed as they wrestled with the problem and its solution.

There was not any immediate, nor visible, risk now that the Hunti had been destroyed and neither Tarkin nor Thesso could sense the strange old man that often showed up where the Chest was or had been. He seemed to have disappeared. Could Tarkin simple hold it once more? At the end of all these discussions, they decided to go over the sea trench idea once more. So far it seemed the best idea they had, but they could wait to go over it again. They needed to make the correct decision. Thesso shared the idea with Francesca, Jodaw, Jakeus, and Josepheos and asked them to mull it over in their ancient minds to check out its viability.

While Thesso and Tarkin were deliberating on this they sensed a group of giants walking towards them and recognised them as the Metungians, that had been caught years and years ago when the Portal was first closed, long before Tarkin was born. The longevity of the Metungians meant they knew how they had arrived on this land and how they had been trapped. They had made a great community for themselves in the mountains choosing to stay hidden deep in their mountain home, cut off from the rest of the world. The other inhabitants of Pardow knew of these cities in the mountains, and of the Metungians. Their isolation and their reputed size and strength ensured they did not get disturbed. The Metungians knew of the Portal, and what it could do, but they had not realised it had been reopened a hundred or so years ago.

Tarkin was a bit surprised to see the huge men and women approaching them. As they came closer, he and Thesso exchanged thoughts, 'Metungians!' Thesso informed Tarkin, they were trapped here at the first closure of the Portal. They are looking to find out what had been taking place these last few weeks. Thesso glided along in the ocean, the men had seen him but seemed unafraid. Tarkin dived off Thesso's head and swam to shore, he walked along the beach to meet the men. He was dwarfed by the huge man that walked forward to greet him. Yanji stopped directly in front of Tarkin and patted him on the shoulder in form of greeting. 'Are you Tarkin?' he asked. Tarkin nodded in agreement. 'Yes, I am Tarkin,' he answered. Tanir stepped forward and said, 'I have been serving with Elgrade in the battle we fought over the dragons, I am Tanir keeper of the mammoths, that you call war beasts. I was sent out after our army retreated to find the beasts, if you will remember they were terrified and they had stampeded, trying to escape the battle. I did not find all of them, and I returned to my homeland after freeing them. I did not feel that they should return to captivity.'

Tarkin asked what they were seeking, and Charlotte said they wanted to know what was so important that such an eclectic, but amazing group, was called to fight the battle against King Elgrade of Cam. 'We saw the dragons flying over the mountains and saw the dust of the battle in the distant. Tanir has returned to us and told us of the battle and the individual groups that were there fighting together. As we live in isolation from the other inhabitants of this world, we do not always know what is happening and we need to know what is, or was, so important and how this may affect us Metungians.'

Tarkin conferred with Thesso as to what to say in reply, 'Can I tell them of the Portal or just the dragons escape.' Thesso answered him at once, 'Perhaps we should tell them of the Portal and note their response as it may have some influence on our decision as to what we have to do with it.' Tarkin agreed with him and invited the group to sit on the beach with him or if they wanted to, go into Ainslea for refreshments and shelter before they talked. 'We are happy here.' 'We have food and drink with us for the journey. And indeed,

I do not think you have a chair or a shelter big enough for us,' Yanji replied aloud. Tarkin grinned back at him as they sat on the beach with Thesso close to the shore to join in when needed.

Tarkin began to explain, 'It was complicated and mixed-up war; the short version is the dwarves of Christiana set free the dragons of Cam, and King Elgrade of Cam wanted them back.' He went on to tell them how everything to do with the war had played out then added. 'But unbeknown to Elgrade or Paelion the dwarf King of Christiana, the dwarves had found a Chest that held the Portal between worlds, the very Portal that brought you all here. They had dug up the small but ancient Chest while mining and had sought the dragons for information on opening the Chest. They did not have any idea it contained something so valuable and dangerous as the Portal. The dragons knew what it was but did not tell the dwarfs, they wanted to get the Chest to Thesso as soon as possible so that he could take care of it.' He paused to see if they had grasped what he was telling them, 'Go on,' Yanji said.

'None of these knew about an energetic being called the Hunti, the Hunti had been the reason the Portal had been closed the second time and caused the problems that forced it to be closed the first time. That was when you were trapped here. The Hunti were pure evil and fed on all sorts of negative emotion but especially pain and grief. They were after the Chest and as soon as the dwarves exposed it, they had felt it and had begun to search to find it. They finally found the battlefield and Tanir. This is what you experienced the at first meeting of the armies.

You could not see, these energies, therefore you could not defend yourselves. Luckily for you the dragons had previously found that the Hunti could not survive fire, and they came to your rescue that day. With the Elves' help as well as Tarkin's family's help they were able to destroy large numbers of the Hunti. Yes, they were fighting against Elgrade's army and the Hunti that day' He smiled 'I can see why Tanir described the battle as complicated and confusing.' Tarkin continued, 'To shorten the rest of the story, let me just say that Thesso and his fellow guardians of the oceans have destroyed those that were left of the Hunti as they fled the battle. Now Thesso and I have the Chest with the Portal inside, hidden in a safe and secure place, so we must decide what to do next. Do we destroy it, do we hide it again, and do we reopen it, before hiding or destroying it, to send you back to Metumia if you desire to go?'

THE DECISION
TO REOPEN
THE PORTAL

Charlotte and Yanji stared at Tarkin and then turned around to see if their fellow Metungians understood what was being offered to them. This was a big question and one that was unexpected, they had long since given up any thoughts of returning to their old home on Metumia They had never imagined this day would come. They would need to return to their mountain home and consult with all their people before any decision could be made. Charlotte asked if there was a limit on the time they had, and after consulting with Thesso, Tarkin suggested two weeks was the deadline. They would have to make up their minds quickly.

The Group of elders did not linger long in Ainslia, and it was a very excited group that returned to their mountain home, they travelled fast as they wanted to get home to talk things over with those they loved and to see what the decision would be. They debated as they hurried along as to whether the decision needed to be unanimous, whether it would be, all should go, or none should go or could groups and individuals decide for themselves. It was certainly a life changing event and could not be taken lightly.

Today's group was young and had been born here on Pardow, so they never knew their home planet, they did not have a hometown of city to go to. The younger of them did not know what a city was, they had heard stories, but they did not understand. They did not have the same ties to it as the elders did, could families be split up with members choosing to go and others to stay? Should they go home as the elders called it? Would they be better off there? Could they fit back into a society that was far more advanced than their own here in the mountains? Their life here was great but it was limited, but this was only if you had knowledge of what was available on Metumia. They wondered if all the inventions and the technical prowess were really needed. They had done well here and lived very well. There was no poverty on the mountain. What if they went home and hated it. What if they were ostracized, would those who left loved ones, just for the day, find them alive and happy to have them back. Would it cause trouble as undoubtedly, they were all presumed to be dead. Is it possible to go back a hundred years and pick up where you left off.

As the group approached the deep crater that formed the boundary of their mountain home, they had come to no conclusion as to what was the best thing to do, they still had so many thoughts and questions running blindly through their heads with no answers coming forward.

A large group had run out to meet them, attracted by the returning party s hurried arrival. They were travelling at haste and were openly agitated and excited. Immediately the Elders arrived they reassured the village that all was well, and no danger followed them home. Immediately they instructed everyone to go home and bring the whole valley to the meeting room, it was urgent, and all were asked to come. Even the ill or wounded should be carried to the assembly. It took a while for all to get settled and to be quiet enough for Yanji to address them. He told them of the events of the day before and what had been offered to them by the Sea Dragon. Yanji wished he had not mentioned the sea dragon because the Metungians began to laugh and taunt him and ask if the group had been imbibing forbidden drinks or herbs. It took a while for everyone to listen and even longer for them to understand what had been said. Great excitement and then concern, and lots and lots of questions, after a considerable time when the conversation was going around and around in circles, Charlotte called halt to the meeting she said, 'Let us all go and talk and think all of this over, try to have a clearer idea of what you will do when asked to vote, we will come back and talk again tomorrow. Same time same place.'

While the Metungians travelled home to discuss what to do about staying or going, Tarkin and Thesso talked about what other groups may wish to go home, he knew there were varied species in Cam but was not sure where and how many there were. In fairness to everyone throughout the land they decided to send out messengers to announce the Portal and that this chance to return to your home planet, or world, or dimension was being offered. Thesso spoke by mind transfer to Josepheos and asked him to inform all the citizens of Cam of this opportunity.

Josepheos set out to talk to King Elgrade as quickly as possible, despite the loss in the battle Elgrade was feeling okay, he had come out of the whole thing looking better than he had hoped thanks to his quick thinking and his announcement regarding the dragons being in Cam forever. He was eager to please Josepheos and met with him straightaway as Josepheos had requested. It took time for the dragon to make the King understand what he was telling him but eventually he understood, or at least he agreed that Josepheos understood what he was talking about. He made an announcement immediately while the crowds were still gathered for the celebrations. He felt magnanimous, like this amazing offer was being given by him. Those who had arrived by the Portal knew what he was telling them and went off to make their decision. His citizens had thought he had gone mad with all the stress of the last few weeks, but he did not seem to care. He was happy and he was in control once more. The three dragons left the city and flew off going everywhere they could think of and passed the message to all they found along the way. It was good to give their wings a stretch without someone or something trying to kill them.

Tarkin dismounted, tethered his horse, and followed the tiny creatures into the forest. He sat down on an offered bench made from a fallen, bent tree. It was comfortable. He explained to them just as he had before to the Metungians. Their answer was very quick and decisive. Tomas spoke for the group, 'We have talked about such an event at length, over the years we have spent on this world. We will not return to Tranzia, we belong here now, we live here, and we love our home. Now that King Paelion has granted us all rights to the Enchanted Forest it is even more important that we stay. This is now our land. That is not a small thing to us. We are grateful and thankful for the offer, but it is long decided. We will stay here.' Every tiny head was nodding in agreement. Tarkin sat with the Tranzicons for a long time sharing their decision with Thesso. They both felt this was the right one for them to have made. The Tranzicons had proved themselves to be valuable allies and now friends. Tarkin felt happy they were staying, who knew when he might need their military services.

The two weeks grace period was nearing its end and still the Metungians had not came back with an answer. Others decided to stay here on Pardow but one or two had decided to go back to their home worlds. Tarkin was extremely excited by this news because he knew he would get to escort them back to their homelands; he would get to see their worlds and experience the pleasure of timelessness once again. One of the species that had decided to return to their own world, was the Nerrens. These were the reptilian-like creatures the dwarves had described to him. He had spent time thinking of them and their identity, he had never encountered a Nerron nor had any knowledge of them. Finally, a conversation with Thesso had given him images and details of their old planet and their customs this information was useful, but he was still looking forward to physically meeting one of their members. When the auspicious day was finally here, they arrived on the beach in a group of around fifty, they all wore the same long robes and were carrying woven baskets. There were young and old, some held tiny babies in their arms. Cute little wiggle babies with long thin tails. Their homeland was called Nerra and was in a galaxy an extraordinarily long distance from Pardow. Without the Portal light years would be needed to travel there if there was a means or craft that could take the journey.

Thornfoot had previously shared with Thesso and Tarkin his sighting of the bird-like man at the gates of the city of Cam and now a small group of these beings arrived on the beach, along with the Nerrons Tarkin remembered what Thornfoot had shared with him and when he saw them, he greeted them warmly. In the conversation that followed he learned that they were called Euradi. Tarkin was impressed with their beauty, their feathers were rainbow coloured and iridescent, shimmering in the sun as the wind on the beach rippled through them. They had wings that they kept neatly folded, but when spread out wide were extraordinarily strong and they could fly. Their world was not in a Galaxy but in another dimension which was remarkably close to Pardow, but it could have been a million miles away because the barriers to pass through to get there were impenetrable without the Portal's magic. They had made the difficult decision to return home because their numbers were becoming too small, and they did not wish their species to die out one by one here. They decided to go back to their home in one of the multitude of dimensions that exist alongside our own. They called their home Radi.

The very next day the Metungians walked down from the mountains to the shores of the Eastern Sea, it had taken deep and meaningful debate which had had gone on endlessly throughout the city, but eventually they reached the decision that they preferred to stay here on Pardow. They had based this decision on the fact that they had no idea what was happening now or had happened on Metumia while they were gone. Their life here was good, they had a safe city, they were a part of a strong community and slowly over the years they had been connecting with the rest of the planet. Once this majority decision had been made the remainer of the Metungians made the same decision that they too would stay here on Pardow.

All the individual groups had made their decisions and everyone leaving to return to their home planet or world was assembled on the beach. Thesso swam out to the coral reef and retrieved the Chest along with the Portal. Along with those who had decided to return to their home worlds was an exceptionally large crowd of excited and curious well-wishers and onlookers. Tarkin had sought permission for his three children to travel with him and it had been granted by the hierarchy via Thesso. Karmen, Lase and Eske were overjoyed, they had heard their father's stories for decades, and now they would live one of them. Thesso brought the Chest up on the beach. He and Tarkin joined their minds to open the Chest. Tarkin took the disc in his hand and asked the Portal to open. A vortex formed in front of him, and he invited the travellers to step through. It was a nervous, but happy and excited group that stepped into the Portal. Tarkin held the Portal's entrance stable as his children also stepped inside. Thesso went through the opening next and Tarkin went in last, waving farewell to the rest of his family and to all those watching on the beach. The vortex closed and silently they all disappeared.

The watchers who had gathered out of curiosity to witness the Portal in action wandered off, not knowing how long it would take for the travellers to return to Ainslia. Just hours later, or so it seemed, the Portal reappeared in the exact spot that it had disappeared. Thesso slithered out and directly behind him Tarkin and his children stepped out.

Tarkin was about to close the Portal when he saw a glimmer of movement on one of the pathways, shocked he telegraphed this info to Thesso. By now he could see a large group of a species unknown to him, they were heading his way. How did they get into the Portal and why had he and Thesso not known they were in there.

'Should I quickly close the Portal?' he urgently enquired of Thesso, as now he could clearly see an assortment of unfamiliar species coming toward him. 'No! You cannot do that,' Thesso shouted back to him, 'if you do, they are trapped in the pathway forever or until it is opened again, we have no choice but to let them through.' The group were now at the exit to the Portal and tumbled out onto the beach, laughing and smiling they greeted the stunned onlookers.

As Tarkin stared openly at the newcomers something was formulating in his mind, 'Here we go again!' he thought.

ACKNOWLEDGEMENTS

There is only one person to thank, or hold responsible, for this story and that is Ainslie, my beautiful granddaughter.

ABOUT THE AUTHOR

 awn was born in Western Australia's Mid-west and has lived in most areas of Australia and overseas, in both big cities and tiny country towns. Currently she, and her partner, have purchased a convenience store /café in the Great Southern. Always up for a new challenge and full of enthusiasm they hope to turn it into a destination as well as the community hub it is now.

Along with her writing Dawn is a mosaic artist. She also likes to paint and create Steampunk art and jewellery.

Dawn began writing this book after a challenge from her 13year old granddaughter as to her ability to write a fantasy story. Some 12years down the track the first story of Tarkin and Thesso is complete.

THE END

THORNFOOT
ENTERS AEON

Darkness filled Thornfoot's mind, and he was suddenly weightless, he relaxed into the pleasure that filled him. When he regained consciousness and his senses, he was in a place of indescribable beauty. Realising that he was no longer on Pardow he looked about. He did not feel alarmed as that emotion was not available to him here. He witnessed his fellow warriors entering the field one by one, he greeted these men and dwarves, and they responded to him. He recognised the men he had been in fighting against in the battle just minutes before, or maybe an eternity before, he could not grasp the memory. He felt only a calm acceptance. Where are we? He tried to ask of his companions, but he formed no words for language was not necessary.

They had reached the Realm of Aeon, a boundless, eternal plain where time ceases to exist in any linear form. Neither cold nor warm, neither day nor night is part of this world. There is a kind of glowing twilight, where the sky shimmers with shifting colours like distant auroras. A soft wind moves across the plains, carrying fleeting memories and whispers of lives once lived, of loves, losses, triumphs, and regrets.

Their surroundings are pale silver, or gold, or grey, he cannot decide but knows it is wonderful. The energy around him feels soft to his touch, like mist made solid. Flowers bloom everywhere and he bends to smell them, but they dissolve into the atmosphere which is glowing faintly with inner light.

Souls entering Aeon can remember who they are, but without the weight of pain, regret, or guilt. Now is all there is. They walk freely around, going wherever they please, enjoying the effortless of every need, thought or desire as they please. They do not understand it yet, but they are walking towards a destination,

Their destination here on Aeon is the Lake situated at the heart of the beautiful world. Here and there the inhabitants walk alone. Others are joined by those they loved in previous lives. When they reach the Lake of Mirrors they will find an immense body of reflective water, glistening silver in the sun. This miraculous lake does not reflect your physical image, but it sees you, it reveals your truth. Those who gaze into it see themselves not as they were, but as they are now, complete, unburdened, and eternal.

Aeon is not a place of judgment. It is a place of becoming and of beginning. Numbers will remain here forever, content in the peace and beauty of this serendipitous world. Others, filled with purpose, journey onward into the next cycle of their soul: rebirth, reincarnation, or something beyond even Aeon's reach. Even now Thornfoot walks towards his own destiny:

.